THEIR REIGN

THE RITE TRILOGY BOOK 3

A. ZAVARELLI

NATASHA KNIGHT

Copyright © 2022 by A. Zavarelli & Natasha Knight
All rights reserved.
No part of this book may be reproduced in any form or by any
electronic or mechanical means, including information storage
and retrieval systems, without written permission from the author,
except for the use of brief quotations in a book review.

This is a work of fiction. Names, characters, places and incidents
are either the product of the author's imagination or are used
fictitiously, and any resemblance to actual persons, living or dead,
business establishments, events, or locales is purely coincidental.

ABOUT THIS BOOK

Their Reign is Book 3 of The Rite Trilogy. The books must be read in the following order:

His Rule
Her Rebellion
Their Reign

The Rite Trilogy is set in the world of The Society. It is the story of Mercedes De La Rosa and Judge Montgomery and the trilogy can be read as a standalone series.

If you're new to The Society and would like to read the first series of books in the world, you can start with Requiem of the Soul. You can find more details and store links by clicking here.

1

JUDGE

I hold Mercedes's shoe in my hand and free the fabric of her dress from the post. There was no one in the woods. I knew there wouldn't be. I look around the deck for traces of blood and am relieved when I don't find any. Taking my phone out, I scroll to Santiago's number and step back inside.

"Get some men out here," I tell Raul as Santiago's phone rings. I look around at the destruction indoors, walking through the living and dining rooms to the hallway and up the stairs to her bedroom. The phone goes to voicemail, so I disconnect. I'll try again in a few minutes. He's probably sleeping.

In the closet, the stack of shoeboxes is undisturbed. She never even got to where she'd stashed the money. The bed has been made since the last time I was here but otherwise, the bedroom is untouched. In the bathroom, there's an overturned makeup bag. A tube of mascara that's rolled under the pedestal sink. Her various perfume bottles are intact, though. All lined up neatly along the counter.

I study that, finding it odd. The mirror isn't smashed. I expect it to be. I recall the television downstairs hadn't been touched either.

Back in the bedroom, the laundry basket of men's clothes I'd seen when I'd first come here is gone. Georgie probably came by to pick it up at some point.

On my way downstairs, I notice how one of the framed photos along the wall is crooked, but the rest are straight. I adjust it and look at the picture. It's the three of them, Georgie, Solana, and Mercedes, in one of their aerial yoga classes.

Once downstairs. I walk into the kitchen. I hear Raul talking on the phone calling men in. A beautiful vase of multicolored tulips stands on her kitchen table. The bright morning sun settles on them. There must be two dozen flowers, and they're fresh.

I turn and face the rooms, noticing how the couch cushions have been upended, and the coffee table is on its side, but the large sculpture of a ballerina lacing up her slipper is still standing in its place, untouched. It's a pretty piece. There's a stack of hardback books beside her. I can tell they've been artfully placed.

"Sir," Raul says.

Puzzled, I turn to him.

"They're on their way," he says.

"Thank you." My phone rings, and I look down to see it's Santiago and answer.

"Judge, you called?"

"Oh, yes," I take in those books again, the ballerina, the pretty flowers in their vase. "Apologies, Santiago. It was accidental. I hope I didn't wake you."

"You're sure? It's not like you to accidentally call me."

"I'm sure. I'm still a little out of sorts I guess."

"Alright. Good night." Santiago keeps strange hours. Ever since the explosion that disfigured him, he has lived in the dark. Until Ivy, at least. Mercedes adjusted her schedule, staying up until all hours and sleeping the mornings away until I broke her of the habit.

"Good night, Santiago."

After disconnecting the call, I walk toward the counter dividing the kitchen from the living room and dip my fingers into the small potted basil plant. The soil is moist. Georgie and Solana have been taking turns watering the plants. The man I have checking the house once a day has seen them come and go. I haven't stationed anyone to remain on site. I didn't think it was necessary.

But I did install a camera.

And as I reach up to pick up the innocuous little

eye from the highest shelf, I see the little red light still blinking. Still recording.

"Raul, can you stay here until the men come? I need to go to my office."

He clearly finds that strange but nods.

I switch the camera off, drop it into my pocket and walk out the door, my panic upon arrival changing, morphing into something else. Anger. Betrayal.

The fresh lashes burn with the heat of it, and when I climb into the driver's side of the car, my breath hisses at the contact of the seat and my raw back. I start the engine and drive to my office, dialing a number as I do.

"Councilor Hildebrand's office," his secretary says.

"This is Judge Montgomery. Is the Councilor in?"

"Yes, sir. Just a moment."

Within a few moments, I hear a click and then Hildebrand comes on the line. "Judge. How are you?"

I don't hear concern. More curiosity. I wonder if he watched the recording they always make to keep a record. Wonder if he enjoyed what he saw. I neither like nor trust Hildebrand. But I understand him. Men like him. And I know how to maneuver around them.

"I've been better," I say.

"Yes, I suppose you have. You should have let her take her medicine. She earned it, and you know it."

"Let's put it behind us."

"It wasn't appropriate, Judge. You, a Sovereign Son."

"And she a Sovereign daughter, let's not forget."

He ignores me. "A future Councilor yourself."

"There isn't even a body yet. Your counterparts may find the topic disagreeable considering the circumstances of any future appointment to The Tribunal."

He chuckles. "Montrose is close to eighty. How much longer do you think he'll hold on to his seat?"

Hildebrand is nearing sixty as far as I can guess. "Let's have that discussion another time."

"How are you, though? I saw some of the footage. He was... brutal."

"As I expect he was instructed to be."

He clears his throat. "I need to be in court in a few minutes. What can I do for you, Judge?"

"Tell me Vincent Douglas's location."

"Now, I'm not sure that's a good idea. I would hate to see the same thing happen to him as did his sister. That's not who we are as a Society. Besides, Ms. De La Rosa more than earned her punishment, and I'll remind you that you *chose* to stand in her place. If this is about vengeance, I cannot assist you."

It's my turn to chuckle as I pull into the parking lot of the courtroom where my office is located. "No, Councilor. I am not interested in vengeance. I'd like to know his location so I can be assured Ms. De La Rosa is safe."

"He will not come after her. He gave me his word."

"Well, then by all means, if he gave his word, let's close the matter."

"Don't be flippant."

"Where is he?"

"Answer me a question, and I will do the same."

Calculating bastard. I climb out of the car and lock it. "What do you want to know?"

"Why did you do it? Why invoke Vicarius? No one has in my lifetime. And for you to do it for her, a woman who is not your family, not your blood, not anything to you."

Ah. But therein lies the crux of it all.

She is not merely something to me.

She is everything.

I stop walking, as if just realizing it myself. Because Mercedes was right the night I told her about Theron. About my fears. I am an idiot. I have feelings for this woman. Powerful feelings. Even as I know and have always known that a wife was not in the cards for me. A family of my own would always be denied me. The stock I come from would not allow for that. I know it. My grandfather knew it. And I'm pretty sure it's why Councilor Hildebrand is in such a rush to get me seated on The Tribunal. He sees my potential.

"Judge?"

I blink, then draw a breath. "In all honesty, Councilor, I would not submit her to your cruelty."

"Hm."

"You and I, we understand one another," I continue. "We always have."

"Yes, we have. I wonder how the power of a Councilor of The Tribunal will corrupt you when the time comes, Judge. I look forward to watching your progression."

"You mean my deterioration."

He ignores that. "You have it in you. Carlisle knew it too. When it is time, we will make a powerful team, you and I."

I clench my jaw. "You asked, and I answered. Now answer my question."

"Vincent Douglas was escorted onto a flight to Reno, Nevada, late last night. Whether or not he remained there is no longer a matter for The Tribunal."

I disconnect the call, relieved and irritated at once. How well does he know me? Better than I guessed? As well as my grandfather? He and Carlisle were close. They would have discussed their vision for The Tribunal, the most powerful institution within IVI.

I enter the office, which is empty, and I realize it's because it's the weekend. I'm grateful I don't have to see anyone and head directly into my office, where I lock the door and sit behind my desk. I turn on my computer, plug in my password, and navigate to the app connected to the security camera I installed in Mercedes's condo.

And I watch.

I watch as a masked intruder enters from the patio door. I peer close when he fills the screen, taking in his height and build. Tall and powerful, he tears her place apart. Sort of. He takes a call, checks his watch, then disappears. I wish I'd set up more cameras because he's out of sight for a while. I move the recording forward until early evening when I was in a dungeon of The Tribunal being whipped. Mercedes enters the living room, her steps slow, one hand over her mouth as she takes in the wreckage.

And if I didn't know better, I'd believe she was surprised. Especially when the masked man comes back into view and grabs her from behind. She screams. I can tell from her face. She fights him, stomping on his expensive shoes. I recognize them. He whispers something in her ear, and she pauses, then she fights him all the way out the patio door, even losing her shoe in the process as he carries her off the screen.

"Motherfucker."

When I get my hands on them, I'm going to fucking kill them.

2

MERCEDES

"**G**et off me!" I scream, thrusting my palms against the man as he tries to maneuver me into the back of a van.

"Mercedes," he hisses under his breath. "You can stop with the dramatics now. I think you've been convincing enough."

Something about his voice makes me pause, but before the full weight of understanding settles over me, he hauls me into the back of the van and slams the door shut.

"Go!" he bellows at the driver.

"Georgie?" His name leaves my mouth on a broken whisper.

"Yes, Jesus." He rips off his mask and tosses it onto the floor as the van lurches forward. "I think your Oscar-worthy performance back there will leave permanent scars on my arm.

He pulls up his sleeve to examine the damage while I try to make this situation make sense. My eyes move to the driver. She's wearing a hooded cloak and big black sunglasses, but I'd recognize those red nails anywhere.

"What the hell is going on?" I demand. "Why are you and Madame Dubois kidnapping me?"

Georgie blinks, his gaze moving over my face before he sucks in a sharp breath. "Did you not read your text messages?"

Text messages? I glance down at my dress, realizing I don't even have my phone.

Georgie mutters a curse and produces the burner phone from his pocket. He must have grabbed it in the scuffle. When he pulls up the screen and checks for himself, his brows draw together, and then his gaze snaps to mine.

"Jesus, babe, you really didn't know? Oh my god." He pulls me in for a hug, and I release a long breath.

"What is going on?" I ask.

"Solana texted you," he explains. "We have a plan to help you hide. God, sweetheart, you must have been so terrified. I thought you knew, and you were just laying it on thick."

I half laugh, half cry before I pull back to look at him and shake my head. "I didn't know. I was just focusing on getting to the condo, and the next thing I know, you're abducting me."

He nods in understanding and then slowly eases

me onto a bench seat, giving my hand a squeeze before he releases it and sits beside me. It's at about this point it occurs to me I still have no idea where we're going or what's happening.

"You didn't need to do this," I tell him. "I have cash at my place. I was just going to grab it, and—"

"No, you don't," Georgie interrupts solemnly. "He took it."

It's impossible to miss the disapproval in his tone, and I don't have to ask who he's referring to. Of course, it could only be Judge. He didn't want me to have any means of leaving.

I swallow and dip my head as that news settles over me. I don't know how I'm supposed to feel about that, but my gut tells me this isn't good.

"Oh, God." I bring my trembling fingers to my forehead, pressing them against the rising tension. "What am I going to do? They're never going to let me go."

"It's okay." Georgie rubs my back. "We have a safe space for you. We'll keep you there until we can figure something out."

I smile through my tears because he sounds so determined. But Georgie doesn't yet understand there's no such thing as a safe place for me. He knows about The Society now, but he can't possibly comprehend their power. The full depth of their reach is suffocating, yet this is the only option I have because Santi and Judge have stripped me of any others.

"Thank you," I tell Georgie, and I mean it. "This will just be temporary. I'm not going to burden you guys forever."

"Honey, you are not a burden," he assures me. "Never."

When I don't respond, he stops rubbing my back and gently turns my chin to face him.

"Say it with me," he insists. "You are not a burden."

I don't want to because it feels like a big fat lie, but I know Georgie, and he won't drop this until I give in, so I say it.

"Good girl." He grins, rather pleased with himself for my capitulation. "This is what friends are for. We ride or die, baby."

"I don't know what I did to deserve a friend like you." I reach for his hand and give it a squeeze. "Because I'm pretty sure none of my Society friends would ever stage a kidnapping to help me."

"Mm-hmm, that's called next level, sweetheart. Don't you forget it."

I laugh despite being so exhausted and emotional I can't think straight. And then the van pulls to a stop, and Madame Dubois turns off the ignition.

"How'd you get her to help with this wacky plan?" I ask.

"Are you kidding?" Georgie snickers. "She's the one who showed up with the mask and a van this morning. There was no asking."

Again, I laugh, and I feel better just knowing Georgie is here with me, even for a little bit. He helps me up and opens the rear door, and when we step outside, we both freeze.

"Holy shit." I stare at the home we're parked in front of, wide-eyed. "What is this place?"

Georgie seems equally awestruck by the elegant villa with Greek-style columns, a beautiful courtyard, and gardens that must cost a fortune to maintain. Madame Dubois, on the other hand, is as casual as ever as she saunters up to the door, snapping her fingers at us to follow along.

"Who knew psychic work paid so well," Georgie mutters.

"Oh, no." Madame Dubois turns to him with a twinkle in her eyes. "The pay is absolute shit, but that's not why I do it. I'm very wealthy. Old family money."

With that information bomb, she turns and unlocks the door, then gestures us inside. We follow her, and I quickly find that while the outside is stunning, the interior is even more so. There's a very French style to the home with herringbone floors, gold accents, and ornate crown molding as far as the eye can see.

"This is amazing." My fingers trail over the beautiful marble console table in the entryway. "I can't believe you live here, Madame Dubois."

"Oh, I don't," she answers with a wave of her hand. "It's just one of my properties. I spend most of my time at an apartment in the French Quarter. But don't worry, this one's under a business holding. It won't be traced back to me."

She sounds certain, but I'm not. I know with Judge's resources he'll probably have someone tailing Solana and Georgie within hours.

I swallow and turn to him. "You aren't staying here with me, are you?"

He offers me a sympathetic smile and shakes his head. "No. Unfortunately, for this plan to work, we both need to get back for when the cavalry comes."

"You shouldn't have to deal with that." Guilt chokes my voice. "This isn't fair to you."

"Mercedes, please." Georgie rolls his eyes. "If Judge brings along those guards he's been rolling with, I will gladly consent to a pat down. I would make that sacrifice for you."

He's trying to be funny, but I can't laugh. I know the guards won't hurt them, but they can make their life very difficult. And Judge especially.

"I should go," I tell them both. "Then you really won't have any idea where I am or—"

"Nonsense, child." It's Madame Dubois who shuts down my protest this time. "I've withstood far worse than the likes of armed men. Let them come. I will gladly welcome the challenge."

Oh god, I don't want to put them through this. I feel like I'm going to hurl again, but I know that's not possible because I haven't eaten anything.

"Go." Georgie grabs my shoulders and urges me toward the stairs. "Take a bath. Eat something. Then get some rest. We have a woman coming to pick you up in the morning at eight. She will take you to your doctor's appointment."

My head swims with this information, but they don't give me time to argue further. Georgie releases me, and they head for the door, pausing to set my burner phone and a house key on the table.

"Use the numbers we gave you to contact us," he says. "And don't worry if you don't hear back right away. I'm sure your lawman will be breathing down my neck by morning if he's not already at my house."

"We have time yet before he comes," Madame Dubois answers with a knowing glint in her eyes. "Don't worry so much."

I nod carefully, and without another word, they open the door, step outside, and leave.

THE HOUSE, WHILE BEAUTIFUL, QUICKLY BECOMES empty. After giving myself a tour, opening every door and inspecting each room, I was relieved to find that I was, in fact, safe here. At least for now.

I took a shower, ate one of the prepared meals from the fridge, and then wrapped myself in a cashmere blanket and stared at the wall.

Time passes. Exhaustion settles over me, but I can't stop thinking about what I've done. I find myself playing every possible scenario over and over in my mind. I think about Judge's reaction once he realizes I'm gone. Will he be hurt? Or more likely, will he be relieved that I did the thing he couldn't?

I don't know which possibility is more agonizing, but I know one thing. If he does find me, he will be angry as hell. Santiago too. I will have embarrassed them by running away like a coward. A De La Rosa doesn't run from their problems. They face them head-on. Only, this time I can't. Because what I'm facing feels like a firing squad, and I'm backed against a wall.

I appreciate Georgie and Solana helping me this way, but I know I can't stay here long. Not really. I don't have any cash now, and that's a problem, but I'll have to leave regardless. Maybe I can hitch a ride to another city and stay in a shelter until I can figure something else out.

As I consider it, I cringe at the insanity of that plan. I wouldn't be safe in a shelter. I won't be safe anywhere. Not once the full power of IVI is on my trail.

I draw in a shuddering breath, pull the blanket up over my head, and sink deeper into the couch. I'm too numb to cry anymore. I'm too tired to do anything. So I close my eyes, and despite all odds, I fall asleep.

3

MERCEDES

Something jolts me from my sleep, and my heart ices over in terror as I drag the blanket from my face.

Bang. Bang. Bang.

The knocking on the front door comes again, and my phone buzzes on the coffee table beside me. When I glance at the screen, I see that I've missed a few calls from Solana. But it's the time on the display that reminds me I was supposed to be up and ready for my appointment.

"Shit." I drag myself upright and stagger toward the door, rubbing the sleep from my eyes.

There's a wicked kink in my neck from sleeping on the couch, and my entire body feels achy and stiff. I can already tell this isn't going to be a good day, and the nausea swirling in my stomach really doesn't help either.

With the morning light comes the clarity that I didn't imagine the events that transpired yesterday. I'm not dreaming but instead trapped in a nightmare I can't seem to escape. I have no money. Very few resources. A man who undoubtedly wants to strangle me for leaving, not to mention one who really does want me dead. And then there is the matter of The Tribunal and the consequences awaiting me should I be recaptured.

All these thoughts weigh heavy on my shoulders as I schlep my way to the door. It doesn't get any better when I open it to find an unfamiliar face staring back at me.

"We're late." The woman huffs at me. "We have to go if you want to make the appointment."

Crap. I'm not in any sort of state to be presentable, but I know Georgie and Solana went to a lot of trouble to set this up. With my current circumstances, this might be the only chance I have to visit the doctor for a while.

"Give me five minutes," I tell her apologetically.

She smacks her gum in annoyance, her eyes moving over me. "Rough night, huh?"

The way she says it makes me think she has no clue that I'm pregnant and not hungover. Whoever she is, it's clear she doesn't know Georgie or Solana. She's just a hired driver.

"Yeah, something like that," I mutter. "I'll be right out, okay?"

She nods and traipses back to her car, and I shut the door and dash into the bathroom. Luckily, Georgie thought of everything, so I have some toiletries to use and some of Solana's clothes. I change into a pair of leggings and a T-shirt. Then I make quick work of washing my face, brushing my teeth, applying deodorant, and pulling my hair back into a ponytail. It's not the best I've ever looked, but it will have to do.

When I head for the door, I grab the house key Georgie left sitting on the console table and meet the driver out at her beaten-up Kia. She's propped against it, smoking a cigarette while she waits, but quickly snuffs it out once I approach.

She even opens the door for me, which is almost laughable, but when I arch a brow at her in question, she just shrugs. "I'm getting paid good money for this gig. Expect high-class service."

I smile despite my grim mood and lower myself into the passenger seat.

The driver, whose name I learn is Nikki, fills me in on her obsession with K-pop for the duration of the journey. Meanwhile, I check the rearview mirrors and scan the road for a black Rolls Royce. When I don't see anything, I skim through Solana's messages from this morning and read her instructions for the doctor's appointment. It's all very spy-like, and they seem to have thought of everything. I would be more impressed if I wasn't slightly hyperventilating at the thought of getting caught any second.

Nikki's car screeches to a halt in front of a private doctor's office, and she wrinkles her nose when she reads the obstetrics and gynecology sign.

"I guess this is the place, huh?" She pulls a cigarette from her pocket and shoves it between her lips. "Have fun in there. I'll wait outside."

"Thanks." I get out of the car and walk inside in a daze.

I'm not convinced Solana's instructions are actually going to work, but when I reach the front desk and tell them I'm here to check in under the name of Kelly Williams, the receptionist doesn't question it.

"We've already received all your paperwork," she tells me. "And it looks like you're cash pay... and that's been taken care of too. So you can go ahead and have a seat."

I do exactly that, and while I'm sitting there, a few of the other women in the waiting room glance at me like I just crawled out of a drug-fueled rave. I can't exactly blame them because I know I look like hell, but their judgment really isn't helping my nerves.

Luckily, it doesn't take long for a nurse to come and retrieve me. In the privacy of the exam room, she goes through the motions of getting my vitals and asking me a few questions while she types my responses into a tablet.

Once that's finished, she instructs me to get on the table and get comfortable, as if that's possible, informing me the technician will be in shortly.

I'm lying there staring at the ceiling when the tech comes in and greets me. I have another moment of panic as she gets to work, applying gel to my belly and explaining what she'll be doing today. I don't hear much of it. I'm just trying to focus on breathing because things are getting way too real.

It comes over me as the wand starts to move, and the noise becomes background to my racing thoughts. I'm going to be a mom to an actual baby, and I have no idea how I'm going to take care of either of us.

"It's okay to be nervous..." The tech's words drift off as I drag in a hollow breath.

Jesus, I have no idea what I'm doing with my life. There's going to be a tiny human relying on me. And truth be told, I don't have the faintest clue how to be a good mother. My mother was decent, but she didn't have a clue either, if I'm being honest. I know this because our housekeeper Antonia was the one who practically raised us.

"Oh, fucking hell," I curse as tears spring to my eyes.

"Hey, it's okay." The tech pauses, and I feel like an idiot for crying in front of her. "It's a very emotional time. I know it's a lot, especially for a first-time mom, but you're going to do great. I always joke that it's better to get it out of the way with two babies in one go. Sink or swim, right?"

I stop, blink, and stare at her as I sniffle. "What do you mean two babies?"

"Twins." She furrows her brow as if she's wondering if she needs to call in a psych eval. "You're having twins."

My eyes snap to the screen, and for the first time, I realize it's not just static I'm hearing in the background of my thoughts. It's actual heartbeats.

"Oh, my god," I whisper.

"Oh, my god, yay?" she asks hesitantly.

I take a moment to absorb the news, and my head feels like it's in a cloud, but at the same time, warmth expands from my chest, slowing my breathing and bringing me back to earth.

"Can you show me?" I lean up on the pillow to get a better look.

She smiles way too big and then nods enthusiastically, moving the wand around to show me. After a moment, when I blink away the tears, I can see the outline of two heads and two vague body-like shapes.

My heart stops. And then it starts again. And I'm crying in earnest now, but for a whole different reason.

"Twins," I murmur in disbelief. "I'm having twins."

"Yes, ma'am," the tech chirps happily. "And it looks like you're just shy of four months along."

Holy crap.

Four months. Has it already been that long?

I look down at my belly, and from this position, the protrusion is way more obvious than it's been hidden under my oversized dresses. If anyone were to see me in a pair of pants and a regular shirt, there would be no possibility of hiding it. But honestly, I don't want to. Not anymore.

I understand that as my hand hovers over what will be my babies' home for the next five months. God, that's way too soon. Yet it's not soon enough.

My emotions are high when the doctor comes in and gives me the confirmation that I have two healthy babies growing inside me. She hands me a list of guidelines for pregnancy, and the tech gives me a towel to clean up. Then with the photo evidence in hand, I'm sent back out into the world with the undeniable truth hanging above my head.

I'm carrying not one but two of Lawson Montgomery's stubborn little monsters inside me.

4

JUDGE

I pull onto the drive of Ezra's home office and park. The main house is dark. His wife and three girls are asleep, safe and sound in their beds. It's past midnight. Climbing out of my car, I head to the building set farther back from the drive. It's made to look like a smaller version of the house itself.

"Judge," he says when I enter without knocking. He's expecting me. He stands and gestures to the chair in front of the desk. "Sit down."

I take it, scrub a hand over my face. I'm tired. It's been seven days since Mercedes disappeared. Well, since she took off. I've had additional men on Georgie and Solana. Ones they don't know about. I've been to see them both, but they're not cracking. Even though I know for a fact the masked man who carefully trashed Mercedes's house was

Georgie. And neither of them is exactly denying what they did. The glares and strange looks I'd been getting over the last few weeks, though, were nothing to the cool reception I've received from them since.

Neither Georgie nor Solana are criminals, though, and they're not very good at covering their tracks. So far, they've only succeeded at one thing, the most important thing. Hiding Mercedes. Which is the only reason I haven't gone completely mad this last week. At least I know she's safe and not in the clutches of Vincent Douglas who, despite having given his word to Hildebrand, rented a car at the Reno airport and drove straight back to the city. At least I've been able to track him, though.

"Thank you for doing this, Ezra. I am sure you'd rather be in bed."

"It's no problem, Judge. This is a priority."

"You found her?"

He nods, turns his laptop around and brings up a photo of a woman I vaguely recognize although I can't place her right away.

"This woman is known in the Quarter as Madame Dubois." It takes me just one more minute.

"The psychic who has a table at the apothecary?"

"One and the same." He pushes a button, and another image comes up, this one of an elegant woman in a Chanel suit. "Madame Dubois is Claudine Dubois Bernard." He clicks to another photo of her at an event with some sort of European royalty. "Heiress of the Bernard empire."

"Bernard? I'm at a loss."

"High-end leather goods, specialty merchandise. Better known in Europe than here perhaps."

"And she works as a fortune-teller?" I'm confused.

He chuckles. "I'm guessing she's passing the time. Probably having some fun. I hear she's pretty good, though," he says with a grin.

"If you believe in that sort of thing. What does she have to do with Mercedes?"

He turns the laptop around and starts typing again. "I've been able to pick up some conversation between Solana and Georgie about a mysterious M."

I roll my eyes.

"Exactly. These two aren't calculating criminals."

"No, they're not. And I suppose that's a good thing for Mercedes."

"My men noticed they both have two cell phones, but the second phones are burners. I couldn't track much through those. However, in one conversation on the devices I was able to tap into, they discussed the Dubois woman and the fact that they had no idea who she was. That was a few days ago, and it took me a little time to put all this together. Madame Dubois has several properties in the city, but she resides in her French Quarter apartment. I've had men watching the other homes and..." He trails off and turns the laptop around again. "I believe this is Ms. Mercedes De La Rosa under the hat and sunglasses."

I peer eagerly at the shots of Mercedes leaving a beautiful Greek Revival–style mansion late one afternoon in a flowing dress that reaches her ankles. A large black hat and big round sunglasses camouflage her face. Her long, dark hair is loose and blowing in the wind, and it's when we get to the photo when that wind knocks her hat off that I'm sure. I go through the photos again. Even the huge sunglasses can't hide her beauty but accentuate it, and given her height, she looks like a fashion model who has just stepped off a runway.

"What's the address?"

He slides a piece of paper across the desk, and I take it. It's about an hour out of town.

"I took the liberty of having a key made." He hands that over too. "This will let you in from the back door."

I take it and wonder about Ezra and exactly the ties he has. "You are resourceful."

"It's my job," he says. "She's in the house. I've kept two men watching both front and back entrances. She won't go anywhere without us knowing."

"Well..." I stand and pocket the paper. "It won't be an issue because by tomorrow morning she'll be safely ensconced in my home again. Thank you, Ezra."

"My pleasure. I'm glad she's safe."

"As am I."

By the time I reach the behemoth mansion, it's past one in the morning. I see the men Ezra mentioned. They're in unmarked vehicles that blend into the neighborhood. I'm sure Mercedes has been looking over her shoulder, but she has lived a life of privilege, and she's not used to being on the run. She knows what IVI guards look like, but I doubt she'd see these men as a threat in their simpler vehicles that blend into the general population.

The gate around the property is open, the house itself dark. The street is empty. This neighborhood is outside of the touristy part of New Orleans. I walk swiftly toward then through the gate, wondering if it's ever closed, considering how it's dug into the soft, mossy grass. I bypass the front entrance, not worried about the motion detector I trigger on the side of the house. It's not going to alert Mercedes or anyone else. It's poorly positioned where there aren't any windows.

Using the flashlight on my phone to locate the lock at the back door, I slide the key in, turn it, and enter the house. I shine the light over the room. The large, old kitchen has updated appliances and a long chopping block counter with a farmhouse sink. The floors are tile and probably original to the house.

It's a long, relatively narrow kitchen, and I walk the length of it, taking in the single dish in the sink and the teacup still on the counter with its tea bag in it. It's cold to the touch, but the teabag is still damp, so it's probably from earlier tonight.

An old wooden table with seating for six is set in the middle of the room, making it seem even narrower. It's wiped clean. It looks like it's been used for years. I walk through to the formal dining room, take in the antiques, the lace curtains, and although it's messier than I like, I see money here. High-end, well-made furniture, beautiful things in a style fitting to the house and to New Orleans.

On the table by the front door, I see the hat and sunglasses from the photos Ezra showed me. I take careful steps up the staircase to minimize the creaking of the wood as I climb. The bedroom doors stand open. I look inside each one, finding most of the beds stripped of bedding. Which makes sense if Madame Dubois lives in her French Quarter apartment. Quietly, I open a closed door and find it's a bathroom. Like those in the kitchen, the fixtures are high-quality but older, the tiles original, the large claw-footed tub elegant and beautiful. A toothbrush and toothpaste sit on the edge of the single pedestal sink, and the sink is wet from recent use. The towel is askew, and a bath towel is drying on a rack. I pick up the damp bar of soap and see the imprint of the apothecary on it. I recognize it from the items Solana gifted me and remember the elixir she'd given me *for my mood.*

When I bring the soap to my nose, I smell Mercedes. I take a moment to inhale deeply. I can just picture her relaxing in the deep tub and possibly drinking a glass of wine, all while I turn New Orleans upside down to find her.

The lashes I took burn as if fresh. They're healing well, but my movements are slower, and if I stretch too far, I reopen some of the lacerations. I consider what I did. How I stood in her place to save her from having to submit to such a cruel punishment. And I think about her running away, sneaking into the back of Paolo's truck because that's the only way she'd have gotten out. All while I was in that dungeon-like space.

When I imagine her soaking in the tub, relaxing, my hands clench into fists.

I force a deep breath in. I know she ran because she was scared of what The Tribunal would do. What her punishment would be. She may not know the intricacies of the laws, but she does know their ways. I just have to remember that, I tell myself as I walk out of the bathroom and go to the last door at the end of the hall, which is closed. I just have to remember she didn't know what the Vicarius clause was. She has no idea what I endured, or she'd never have run. She'd have been there when I got home. She'd have been waiting for me in my bed.

But all those words go out the window when I open the door and see her in the little bit of light that comes in from the streetlamp through the lace curtains. All those generous thoughts dissipate as I take in her peaceful, sleeping form, long, damp hair fanned out over the pillow, her arm on top of the floral print blanket drawn over her. Her back is to me, and I step closer to the bed to listen to her quiet, soft breathing.

She's sleeping deeply. Soundly. When I haven't slept for days. She's well-rested and freshly bathed, while I have endured cold showers so as not to feel the burn of the lashes that line my back. That will leave scars to last my lifetime.

I close the door and settle into the wingback chair to watch her sleep her last peaceful sleep.

5

JUDGE

It's the middle of the morning when Mercedes finally stirs. I haven't closed my eyes for more than a few minutes.

She rolls onto her back, arching, stretching, feline-like, her arms over her head with a soft, luxurious moan. The birds chirping outside can be heard through the window, which is open a crack. She yawns, covering her mouth, blinking her eyes open momentarily before rolling back onto her side with a sigh.

For a moment, I think she's going to go back to sleep. I wouldn't be surprised. The thought irritates me. But then she bolts upright, sucking in a panicked breath, her eyes huge as they center on me. She clutches the blanket to her chest, and I smile.

"Morning, princess."

The words are barely out of my mouth before

she bolts, throwing the blanket off and scrambling toward the closed bedroom door so fast she's a blur, all dark hair and flowing white cotton gown. She gets to it. Her hand closes over the doorknob. But before she can open it, I strap an arm under her breasts and lift her, tossing her back onto the bed.

"I don't think so, Mercedes."

"Judge, I—"

She takes one look at me as I eat the space between us and lets out a yelp, flipping onto hands and knees to scurry across the bed.

I grab an ankle, tug her back and drape myself over her.

"You what?" I say, fisting her hair and turning her head enough so I'm sure she can see me. "Tell me, Mercedes. You what?"

"I... How..."

I raise an eyebrow. "How did I find you? The better question is how did you think I wouldn't?" I get off her, keeping her pinned with a hand at her back and tugging the nightgown up to her waist. I smack her ass, and she yelps. "That's just the start, little monster." *Smack. Smack. Smack.* I tug her panties down and do it again, three more on the other cheek.

"Let me go!" She kicks her legs, twists and turns as I slide her onto my lap and let loose on her ass, spanking hard enough to leave big red handprints. "It hurts! Stop!"

"What the fuck were you thinking?" I ask over the blows.

"Stop! Judge!"

She's half on her side, trying to escape me while she pulls at the nightgown to cover herself.

"When did you get so fucking modest?" I ask as I rip the fabric away and trap her legs between mine to spank her again, concentrating on her thighs.

"Please! You don't understand!"

"I don't fucking understand? Me? Do you have the first clue what I've been through?"

She doesn't answer.

"Do you?" I spank again, and she cries out.

"It hurts!"

"That's the fucking point, princess." I flip her onto the bed and lift her to her knees. "Do you have any idea what you've put me through? I thought Vincent Douglas fucking kidnapped you! I thought it was him who destroyed your condo and took you. But you're a good actress. I'll give you that."

"It wasn't..."

"Very realistic."

"I swear I—"

I push the goddamn fabric of the too long nightgown away and smack again. "That's how red your ass will stay for the foreseeable future. Spread your legs."

"Judge, I—"

"Spread your goddamn legs."

She does, taking her knees wide. She's on her elbows, looking straight ahead. I take her in. Open. Exposed. She looks back at me.

"Face forward."

"Judge, I can explain."

"I said face fucking forward!" I hear how I sound. How angry. How not like myself.

"Judge?"

"Do what I say, or God help me." I undo my belt buckle, not sure what the hell I'm even thinking because I have no intention of using it on her, and the instant I do, she lets out a scream and jumps from the bed.

"No!" She runs across the room, as far from me as she can get, panic in her wide eyes. She picks up the closest thing she can get her hands on, a small, decorative vase, and throws it across the room at me.

I duck to avoid it, and it crashes against the wall. It shatters and she uses that moment to get past me to the door and slips through my grasp, leaving me holding the fabric of the nightgown when I reach for her. But as the door opens and she charges out, I don't let go and the gown rips, leaving a naked Mercedes stumbling down the hall.

"Get back here!" I go after her and manage to grab a handful of hair to tug her backward. Her arms flail as she falls into me. I catch her, wrap an arm around her, and that's when I feel it.

When I feel the thing that stops me dead.

It's like time stops. The whole fucking world comes to a fucking halt.

"What the—?"

She scurries away when I loosen my grip, and I get a good look when she stands still, letting me.

It takes an eternity to drag my gaze from her small, rounded belly up over her breasts swollen like I'd noticed weeks ago when I'd thought nothing of it, up to her tearstained face.

My mouth falls open as she stares at me, breathing hard.

"Jesus." It's all I can manage.

"I didn't know what they would do. I couldn't let them hurt the baby."

6

JUDGE

Fuck.

I push a hand into my hair. What have I done? What the fuck have I done?

"You don't have to do anything. I know you didn't want this." I have no idea how long we've been standing here. How long she's been talking.

"The pill." They're the only words I can get out. They're the only stupid words I can say.

And those are the ones that stop her. That make her shake her head with a knowing but disappointed set to her mouth.

"I didn't take it. I couldn't."

"Jesus, Mercedes. What the fuck were you thinking?" I'm unable to drag my gaze from her protruding belly, so obvious on her slim frame. How did she hide it from me? She'd been wearing baggier clothes. I'd noticed that but hadn't given it much thought. But we've had sex. I would have felt it. Although she'd been careful, turning away, guiding my hands. It was always dark. Had she made sure of that?

"I won't trap you. It's not what I want."

I shake my head to clear it. She's been talking again. "How far?" My voice is foreign.

"Four months."

"Four months." I push both hands into my hair and pull, stumbling into the wall and wincing when my back hits it. I sink to the floor, draw my knees up and hang my head. Four months. She's four months pregnant with my baby.

"Judge?" She walks cautiously over and kneels at my side. "You're bleeding."

I look at her, see where her eyes move to my shoulder. See the patch of red spreading over my shirt. One of my wounds must have reopened during our struggle.

"What is this?" she asks, touching her fingers to my side, seeing them come away red.

And all I can do is look at her swollen stomach as she kneels there. My baby in her belly. Jesus. What have I done?

"Judge, you're really bleeding badly."

"It's fine," I croak out. I push her hand away and stand. "You need to get dressed." I walk ahead of her into the bedroom and open the closet but don't find anything that belongs to her that I know of.

"Your back!"

I draw in a breath and turn to her. "It's fine. Where are your clothes?"

"It's not fine. Let me look."

"For once, do as I say! Where are your fucking clothes?"

She points at a shopping bag on a chair. I cross the room and take out a long, flowing dress. Now I understand why she stopped wearing her form-fitting clothes. When I take it to her, I can't help my gaze from dropping to her stomach one more time before I pull it over her head.

"Shoes."

She looks around, locates them, and slips them on. A pair of ballerina flats I haven't seen before.

"Let's go." I take her arm and turn her.

"No." She digs her heels in. "Not until you tell me what happened to you."

I search her face, her worried eyes. I can see the protrusion of her belly in the dress now, but only because I know. You wouldn't notice she was pregnant if you didn't know it in these clothes she's been wearing.

"Judge. Please tell me." She reaches a hand to touch my face.

I wince and she pulls away, an expression of hurt on her face.

"You don't have to be afraid of The Tribunal. They won't come after you."

"What?"

"They can't anymore."

"What did you do?" she asks, her voice trembling. A tear slides down one cheek because she knows what I did. What they did. She knows the ways of The Tribunal.

"I did what I had to. We need to go. Now. I need to think."

"Show me."

"No." I try to pull her along, but she resists. I can force her, but I don't want to.

"Show me, Judge."

"You want to see?"

She nods, looking uncertain.

"Are you sure about that?"

She nods again.

Holding her gaze, I unbutton my shirt and slide it down my back. It pulls where it sticks to the fresh blood. Mercedes walks around me.

"Oh god. Oh my god."

I turn to find her eyes wide, cheeks wet with tears streaming down her face. I draw my shirt up as she drops onto the bed, her hand over her mouth.

"Let's go. We need to go." I help her to her feet, and she doesn't struggle. She only grabs her purse as I lead her out to the car and take her home.

7

MERCEDES

"Judge."

I stop in the entryway, peeking up at him from beneath my lashes. I'm half afraid of what I might see in his eyes, but it doesn't matter because he won't look at me. He's staring into the distance, his jaw set, something unreadable in his expression.

He didn't talk to me the entire way home. I know he's thinking about the baby right now... I didn't dare tell him there are two, but I can't stop thinking about his wounds. He took that flesh payment for me. It means something. It means everything. But he's so shut down I can't get through to him.

"Judge, I—"

"Go to your room, Mercedes." His voice is so cold it makes me shiver.

Still, I can't move. I need to fix this somehow. I

need to take care of him, and then I need to make him understand.

He turns his back on me, crimson seeping through his shirt as tension bleeds through his every muscle.

"Go to your room," he repeats. "And if you even think about leaving again, you should know there are guards at every door now. One try, and I'll have you strapped to the bed for days. Do not fucking test me."

He heads down the hall, his shoes echoing in the direction of his office, and I stand there, frozen in silence. A part of me thinks I should listen to him because I've never seen Judge like this. But even so, I can't allow him to suffer. So with more determination than I really feel, I go into the kitchen where I know Lois keeps some first-aid supplies. I grab what I need and gather the courage to go after him.

The door to his office is cracked when I pause outside, and I can see him at the window, sipping from a bottle of scotch. It's a haunting sight and, admittedly, a painful one.

I never once expected him to rejoice in what I'd done. To him, I understand this must feel like another betrayal, one of the worst kind. He never wanted this. He never wanted me. Not in a permanent way. It's a rejection I had braced for, but there's no preparing your heart for something like this.

I push open the door tentatively, and his eyes

move to my reflection in the glass. He goes rigid, and I'm glad I can't see the full spectrum of emotions on his face as I approach him from behind.

Quietly, I set the supplies on the windowsill and draw in a weary breath as I position myself behind him. He doesn't speak when I wrap my arms around him and start to undo his buttons, but his body is so stiff, words aren't necessary to convey his disapproval. Yet he doesn't fight me when I peel the shirt back from one shoulder, carefully removing it from the areas of his back it touches. Judge takes another long pull from the bottle, moves it to his other hand, and then discards the shirt entirely.

For a moment, my sharp inhale is the only sound in the room. Hot tears burn my eyes as my trembling hand hovers over his lacerations, some in various stages of healing, but all of them undoubtedly in the process of leaving scars.

My emotions rush to the surface, tightening my throat as I choke them back. I want to tell him he shouldn't have done this for me. I want to scold him, and at the same time, I want to thank him. Because he saved me. And in some ways, I think I know he always will. Except I can't allow him to do that this time. Not when I've put him in this position. I won't force his hand. I won't force anyone to love me. And I will not make him pay for a decision I made on my own.

With those thoughts in mind, I try to focus on

the task at hand. I reach for the cloths and antiseptic, and I begin the difficult task of cleaning his opened wounds. Judge doesn't make a sound. He doesn't flinch or betray even a second of pain, though I know from experience how badly this hurts. There is no amount of gentility that can take the edge off this kind of agony. Yet he seems to be comfortable with it, as if he's been courting it his entire life. And I realize, in some ways, he probably has.

He told me himself when he confessed his fears. In his mind, he's tainted with bad DNA. He thinks nothing can alter that, and the only way to keep others safe is to keep them at a distance. It breaks my heart, but at the same time, I think I can understand it better than anyone. In many ways, he and I are the same. The only difference is Judge has somehow cracked me open. Now, in place of the hard shell that once protected me is something softer. Something more vulnerable.

The only problem is vulnerability can't be one-sided.

"I need you to know I don't want anything from you," I say the words in a carefully neutral tone while I reapply fresh bandages.

His muscles ripple beneath my fingers, but he doesn't respond.

"This was my decision. I didn't involve you, and I'm not asking for anything from you. Nothing."

Silence.

"I will do this on my own, and I'm okay with that. As far as I'm concerned, you can forget this ever happened. I will talk to Santi, get my inheritance, and step back from The Society. You can go on with your life, and nobody will ever know." My voice wavers slightly at the plan I've mentally prepared, but I steel myself as I go on. "I *want* to do this on my own, so don't feel guilty for the choice I made. I understand you're angry right now, and I get that. But I just need you to know, without a shadow of a doubt, that I want nothing from you. Not a single—"

"Enough." Judge snarls, yanking away from me before I can seal the last bandage.

The ferocity in his tone stuns me into silence, that single word ringing with such finality. But what did I expect? This was always going to be the beginning of the end.

"I'm not going to ask you again, Mercedes. Go to your room."

IT FEELS STRANGE, BEING BACK IN THIS ROOM. MORE accurately, it feels achingly empty. I lie on the bed, staring up at the ceiling, waiting for footsteps I know will never come. But even as pain lances through me and I cry silent tears, I have to believe this is for the best. Judge is angry, and I wish he wasn't, but it serves as a reminder of why I have to follow through with my plan.

I meant what I told him. I'm going to talk to Santi. I've had plenty of time to think about it over the last week, and it's going to be hard. Possibly the hardest thing I've ever done. I'll have to own my choices, and I will do it with my head held high. It won't be a comfortable conversation, given that we've only just started to put the past behind us, but I'm in it now, and there's no getting off this ride. I have to put everyone else's feelings aside and do what's best for my children. No matter what.

Later that night, somewhere between darkness and dawn, I manage to get a little more sleep. I only realize it when I'm awakened by the sound of shouting carrying up through my windows. I sit up, straining to hear what's being said, when I recognize Solana's voice.

Oh, shit.

I'm moving before I can even think it through. I know this isn't going to go over well. Not after they realized I was gone from the house without a word. I didn't even have time to grab the burner phone, so I'm sure they've been going out of their minds with worry. That thought is confirmed when I turn the corner into the entryway and see Georgie and Solana at the door, guards at their sides while they argue with Judge.

"You aren't welcome here," Judge growls, inches away from Georgie's face.

They look like they're about to come to blows, and I don't like this. I don't like it at all.

"Stop!" I yell. "Please, stop."

All three of their gazes whip to me, and Judge shoots me a withering glare so cold, it sucks the breath from my lungs.

"Mercedes." Solana takes a step forward, only for the guard to grab her by the arm. "Are you okay?"

"Quit manhandling her!" I bellow. "Judge, this is ridiculous. Tell him to let her go. This isn't necessary."

"I'm not telling them anything." His jaw sets, and I could almost swear a look of betrayal flashes through his eyes as he turns away.

I don't understand it. Is he pissed at me for taking their side?

"Let her come with us freely," Georgie says, the ire in his voice unmistakable. "Or so help me God, I will make so much noise about this fucking Society of yours you'll wish you'd put a bullet in my head."

"That can be arranged," Judge answers darkly.

"Enough!" I yell at all of them. "Please don't do this."

They all fall silent, and I can see the irritation coiling in Judge's spine, but he still won't look at me. There's no way any of them will handle this amicably with tensions as high as they are, and I have to put them at ease.

"It's okay," I tell Georgie and Solana, taking a careful step forward. "I'm going to be okay here for now. I promise you, I'm safe. I'm going to talk to my brother soon, and we'll get this all sorted out."

"Maybe I should go talk to your brother." Solana's eyes flash with fury as she turns her attention back to Judge. "I'm sure he'd love to hear all about what you've been doing here."

Oh, fuck. My eyes feel huge as her threat settles over us like a dark cloud. If I thought Judge was pissed before, I was wrong. Now, his rage is a living, breathing animal, so palpable I can feel it radiating off him.

"That won't be necessary," I choke out, trying to salvage this trainwreck of a negotiation. "Santi will talk to me."

Georgie looks doubtful that Judge will let that happen, and if I'm being honest, so am I. His current status is throwing off over my dead body vibes, and I know the reason is because he doesn't want to lose Santi as a friend. Solana hit him right in the solar plexus with her well-aimed threat, but in doing so, she also revealed that I've told them far more about IVI than I ever should have. Something I don't doubt will go over too well with Judge.

"I'm not leaving here until I know Mercedes has a line of communication." Solana stares Judge down in a way that I have to give her credit for, considering he terrifies most grown men. "And if one single day goes by that I don't get proof of life, I will burn this place to the fucking ground to find her. Do you understand me?"

I suck in a sharp breath, simultaneously loving my friend and wishing she'd trust my assurances that I can handle this. But then again, I'm the one who dragged them into this world. They only know what they've seen and heard so far, which hasn't been great.

"She'll call you once a day under my supervision," Judge clips out. "At a time of my choosing."

Honestly, I'm surprised by his concession, and I can tell Solana is too. I didn't think he'd cave, but then again, she gave him a powerful motivation. And I'm not sure how to feel about his determination not to let Santiago know what's happening. That doesn't bode well for me.

For a split second, a fleeting thought enters my mind. It's almost too brutal to even consider, yet it's there. Would he try to convince me to get rid of the pregnancy?

As I stare at his profile, I know he couldn't. In my heart, I know Judge. He can be cruel—he said so himself—but I don't believe he'd ever try to hurt me that way. I can't allow myself to believe it for a second. The problem is, I don't know how he thinks he's possibly going to keep this from my brother.

Their Reign

I can shield Judge from The Society. I could live a life separate from them, not attending events. Staying out of the public eye. None of the members would ever have to know these children are his. But I can't shield that information from my brother. There is no way when Santi knows I've been in his care this entire time. It will come out, and it won't end well for their friendship. That, I do regret. But I can't change it either.

"Mercedes." Georgie's voice pulls me back to the matter at hand. "Are you really okay?"

"Yes." I force a tearful smile. "I'm okay."

He gives me a funny look as if he's trying to tell me something, and it takes me a moment to realize what it is. Georgie has always been protective of Solana and me. When we'd go out together, he came up with a system to keep us safe. I had forgotten about it until now, but it's clear that's what he's asking me. We have code phrases we'd use in any situation we ever felt unsafe, and Georgie would handle it. Mine was somewhat of an inside joke. *If only they made a drink that could cure a headache.*

Right now, he needs that assurance. If I use the code phrase in a positive context, he'll know I'm lying about feeling safe here. And I know he won't leave until he trusts that I am.

"Don't worry about me," I tell him softly. "They don't make drinks strong enough to cure a headache, but I doubt I'll need one anytime soon."

His face softens, and Judge turns slightly, shifting his gaze between us, his eyes narrowed. He knows I'm communicating some sort of secret, but he doesn't know what.

"It's time for you to leave," he grits out. "We're done here."

"It will be okay." I mouth the words to them as the guards usher them back, and Judge starts to close the door. "I promise."

8

MERCEDES

Somehow, the absent hours I spend in isolation in my room turn from one day to another until they've blurred together, and I'm not even sure how many have passed. Judge appears at random times in my doorway simply to tell me it's time to call Solana. During these brief interactions, his face is guarded, his emotions completely shut down. I can't tell what he's thinking, but when I follow him down to his office where he allows me to make the phone call, I feel his eyes on me. I've caught him staring at my belly a few times, jaw clenched, eyes somewhere distant. He doesn't give voice to his thoughts, and I'm too much of a coward to ask what they might be.

There are still so many unknowns. How long does he plan to keep me locked up here? When will he let me talk to Santiago? What the hell are we even doing anymore?

I don't know the answer to any of those things. But I know he's not completely immune to me. After the first night I tended to his wounds, it became a silently agreed-on arrangement. With some reluctance on his part, I've continued the procedure every day after I make my phone call. Using some salve I had on hand from Solana's shop, the lacerations have started to heal, and as horrible as it is to see his wounds, a part of me mourns the loss of this last connection between us. Because somehow, I know this is it. Judge doesn't see me the way he once did. I can feel that between us. It's the painful reality I never wanted to face, and now it's impossible to escape.

As I bandage his wounds today, I know too much time has passed. I have to say something. I have to do something. Because I'm going fucking crazy with this ocean of silence between us.

"Are you letting me go to Elena's baptism today?" That's what comes out of my mouth.

The question hangs over the room, heavy and uncomfortable. Beneath my fingers, Judge straightens. He doesn't want me to go, and I know it's because Santi's going to be there. He's afraid I'll tell him today, but I won't. Not on a day of celebration. That will have to wait for another time.

"I'll wait to talk to him," I whisper. "I can arrange

it for another day. I'm not expecting you to be there when I do. I know he'll be pissed for a while, but I think it will be okay. He'll have to see reason. He'll give me my inheritance, and you can finally be free."

"Stop." Judge's harsh command startles me as he shrugs me off and turns to glare at me. "Just fucking stop."

I stare at him in disbelief, and I don't know what to say. This is what he wants, isn't it? Yet he looks so annoyed by the idea that it makes me think maybe he doesn't. At least until he opens his mouth again.

"It isn't your place to talk to Santiago," he growls. "When the time comes, I will do it. Not you."

A surge of anger rises inside me, spilling from my lips before I can stop it.

"No, it's never a woman's place, is it? Not in this fucking world. You want me to leave the decisions about my life to the men. Men who are more concerned with appearances than how I feel. Well, I'm telling you right now, Judge, I'm not going to sit quietly and let that happen. This is my life. My future. And it's not up to you to determine how or when I speak to my own goddamn brother."

"It is up to me." He slams his fist down onto the desk. "You are in my care—"

"No," I bite out. "I'm not in your care. I'm your fucking prisoner. And for what purpose? Why are you keeping me here? What benefit is it to you?"

His nostrils flare, and he rises from his seat so

slowly I know I'm in trouble. I try to take a step back, but his hand whips out and grabs my dress, holding me hostage as he seizes my face in his other palm.

"What benefit is it to me?" He repeats my words, his breath blowing across my lips. "I think the one benefiting here is you, little monster."

Before I can respond, he turns me around and slaps my hands down on the desk while he grinds his pelvis against me. "This is what you wanted, isn't it?"

He pulls up my dress and yanks my panties aside, his palm caressing my ass so gently that it sends a shiver down my spine. "You lured me in with your cunt." He unzips his trousers and grabs a fistful of my hair with one hand while stroking between my thighs with the other. "You took my cock at every opportunity."

I shake my head weakly, though I'm not sure what I'm even protesting. It's the tone of his voice, the coldness. He's being cruel, and I know it's coming. I just don't want to hear it.

"You milked my dick until you got what you wanted." The head of his cock presses against me, and I release a stuttered breath when he pushes inside, settling as deep as I can take him.

The fullness. The pressure. It's so intense. And I want to give in to this feeling, this need. But he's not done talking yet. Not even as he starts to fuck me.

"You stole what I told you I wouldn't give," he

grunts. "And now what, Mercedes? What do you think is going to happen?"

I squeeze my eyes shut, releasing a quiet breath as I try to formulate a sentence. But as he thrusts into me, the only thing I can think about is how much I have missed this. I have missed him. Even in the moments of his cruelty, it still feels sweeter than anything I've ever tasted. I'm already on the verge of coming when his fingers dig into my hip, and he releases my hair to slap my ass cheek.

"Answer me," he growls.

I don't, and he smacks my ass again, harsher this time, his hips colliding against me as he thrusts deep. Fast. Hard.

"Oh god," I whine. "Judge, please."

He slaps my ass so hard I'm on the verge of coming violently, only for him to pull out and ruin it at the last second.

"This isn't for you," he snarls, milking his cock in his fist.

I turn to look at him just as he releases, his come spurting over my ass. There's not an ounce of satisfaction in his eyes. He's doing this to punish me. I realize that when he smears the liquid from his hand onto my skin, leaving me exposed as he tucks himself into his pants and stares down at me.

"Go get ready. We have a fucking baptism to get to."

The car ride to the IVI compound is tense and silent. Judge stares out his window, and I stare out mine. I wish I could say the mood improves when we arrive and I see beautiful little Elena in her christening gown, but it doesn't.

Judge allows me exactly one minute to say hello before pulling me back to stand away from the rest of the gathered crowd. We watch the baptism from a distance, and sadness washes over me as I realize how far away my family feels.

I should be Elena's godmother, but I'm not. Santiago won't grant that to me. It only makes me realize that even though he said we're going to put the past behind us, things will never be the same. I'll never feel like a part of this.

I think the best thing I can do for everyone is leave. Maybe that would make them all happier. Maybe there's a scrap of happiness somewhere out there for me too, but I doubt it. I'm stuck in my feelings when the ceremony ends, and there's a small opening for me to see Elena one last time. I know we aren't staying for the celebration after, and that sucks, but I can tell it's because Judge doesn't want anyone to see what's beneath my dress. He's been on edge the entire time we've been here, his eyes scanning the crowd as if someone's going to notice it at any second. If I don't get out of his hold soon, I know he won't let me go anywhere for fear of someone finding out.

Setting those thoughts aside, I join Santiago and Ivy briefly to offer them my gift, and then I stroke Elena's soft little cheek. It's all I have time for before Judge drags me back out into the courtyard and then back to the prison of his house.

Darkness settles over me, and I curl into myself for the duration of the ride. When we arrive, I don't bother to say anything else to Judge. I don't even look at him as I walk to my room, strip off my clothes, get into the shower, and cry.

9

JUDGE

Betrayed. That is the single word I come to at the end of the day every single day.

She is pregnant. And she has kept it from me knowingly from the beginning. From the moment she didn't swallow the pill she put into her mouth right before my eyes.

I tap Kentucky Lightning and click my tongue. She takes off, galloping toward the jump I barely stopped Mercedes from taking that day so long ago that it feels like another lifetime.

She lives in her room now and I in my study. I go upstairs to my bedroom to shower and change. As much as I don't want to, I often catch myself slowing at her door. And sometimes when I do, I hear her cry quietly. I allow myself to place my forehead against the door. I've even closed my hand over the doorknob. But I've stopped short of opening it. And as I stand there, I let myself feel the agony of it all wash through me. The impossibility. Because there's only one way this can go. And we will both lose.

What the hell did she expect to happen? What did she want out of this? Marriage? I won't. I can't. I swore it to myself a long time ago. Only I know my reasons. She thinks she does, but she only understands the very surface of it all.

But time is running out. I need to talk to Santiago and soon.

After my ride, I hand the horse off to Paolo, who takes him with a quiet nod. The staff knows to stay away from me. My mood is so dark it's as though a pall has settled over the entire house. I go into my study. I should shower first, but I don't. Because I need to make the call. Tell him we need to talk. There's no hiding the pregnancy anymore.

Even though it's before noon, I pour myself a scotch once the door is closed and drink it all. I don't allow her to put the salve on my back anymore. Not since the incident before the christening. Not since I bent her over the table and had her again. There was no pleasure in it though, not for me. Certainly not for her. But there was one thing I said that wasn't quite right. This is my fault. Not hers. I was the one in control. I bedded her. Not coming inside her is an idiotic form of birth control. It's pathetic I ever thought that would work. Because even if the method was foolproof, the draw to come inside her was too strong. And I gave in to it again and again and again.

It just proves my point about marriage. About what I am. Why I can't take a wife or be a father. I am more beast than man. I have not mastered the animal inside me. It's been there all along, quiet, slumbering, one eye open as it patiently lies in wait.

Pouring a second scotch, I swallow it down. I pick up my phone to call my friend, knowing he will probably never speak to me again. I deserve no less. My finger hesitates over the call button. It takes me a long minute to push it.

But before I can even put the phone to my ear, my study door crashes open, and I spin to find a madman at my door. Because that's the only way to describe the expression on Santiago's face. The tension in every muscle in his body. The rage emanating from him is a palpable thing, a thing that swallows up the air in the room and roils as I see what he's holding. The glass box with the once-white sheet inside it. A trophy for Sovereign Sons. The sheet stained with the virgin blood of their wives.

With a roar more animal than man, he sends it crashing against the portrait of Carlisle over the mantel. The box shatters into a thousand pieces, glass and brass and the shame of what I did, what I took, at our feet. My grandfather's face is damaged from the impact, his mouth made to look as though he is grinning.

"How. Dare. You!" Santiago stalks to me.

I stand still. Arms at my sides. Hands fisted. The phone is still inside one. He draws his arm back and delivers a blow so fierce that it momentarily blinds me, sending my head jerking backward.

"I trusted you!" I've barely turned back to him when he does it again, this one catching my temple, making the room spin before I can straighten to take the next one. And the one after that. And the one after that.

"I trusted you, and what did you do? What the hell did you do but betray me!"

My ears ring, and I taste the copper of blood when the next blow to my gut has me doubling over.

"Nothing to say for yourself, you fucking bastard?"

The phone falls to the floor, and I clutch the desk to straighten and face him again.

"Say. Something!"

What can I say?

"Fucking talk, you goddamn bastard!"

"You're right." It's all I can muster because what else is there? I deserve his wrath. I deserve to be punished. That lashing I took in Mercedes's place, it was all a part of this. If I ever believed otherwise, I was a fool. A liar.

He looks at me for a long, long minute, and I see the betrayal in his eyes behind the rage. The pain of learning the truth about someone you thought was better than he is.

I swallow the bile in my throat and open my arms to take more.

And he delivers.

Gripping my collar and hurling me toward the wall, we send a lamp crashing to the floor, the table toppling. He strikes again, the other side of my face this time.

"Fight. Fight you fucking bastard."

"No." The sound is garbled, bloody. "I won't fight you."

He strikes again and again and again, sweat dripping down his face. He's out of breath when he finally stops and stumbles backward. His knuckles are red and raw, and my blood is splattered across his shirt. He wipes the sweat from his forehead with his arm.

"How could you?" His voice is broken too. It's pain I hear now.

"You're right." It takes all I have to look him in the eyes. "I betrayed you."

That seems to send a wave of fresh energy through him, and he begins his attack anew. I don't know if either of us hears the screams for us to stop. I don't know when either of us realizes Mercedes is in the room.

"What are you doing?" She's screaming, wild, her eyes wide, face streaked with tears. "Stop! You're going to kill him."

I look at her. She's behind Santiago, trying to pull him away. He has one hand on my shoulder to keep me up against the wall as he pounds my middle. My ears ring from the earlier hits, and I'm not sure my hearing isn't delayed.

"You're going to fucking kill him!"

"He deserves no less!" He shoves Mercedes back, and she stumbles over the toppled table, falling into the broken glass, screaming as it cuts into her palms.

Santiago stops when he hears her. He turns. And it's when he takes a step toward her that I grab him by his shirt collar and haul him back.

"Not her. You don't touch her!" I throw him sideways, but my desk breaks his fall, and his rage is back. He hurls himself at me, and this time, I do fight him.

"She's not yours!" he spits. "She was never yours!"

Mercedes screams again, scrambling backward as we stumble toward her. "Stop! Please stop!" She's on her feet, and this time, she doesn't try to pull her brother away. Instead, she throws herself between us, into me, clinging with arms and legs around me to shield me from her brother.

My arms wrap around her instinctively, her firm, round belly pressed against mine. My eyes search her face, and my chest aches at the sight of it. Sad and broken. I did this to her. I broke her. She was right. She was never in my care. That was my own arrogance. I made her my prisoner. And I broke her.

Santiago tries to drag her away, but she clings to me. He's forced to release her, and she stands between us facing me, our eyes locked. Silence descends in this war room, a strange quiet passing between us. And I know without a doubt that the end that was coming is here. And that tether between us, that ever-precarious thing that I denied time and again, it has snapped. Gone. Severed for good. She feels it too. I see that much on her face. Hear it in the choked sound as her lip quivers, and she sobs quietly until we're finally interrupted by Santiago's voice.

"Oh, Jesus. Oh, fuck. No."

We both turn to face Santiago because we must. There's a moment when the tips of Mercedes's fingers search for mine, trembling over my thigh until I weave my fingers with hers. We stand, the pair of us, guilty, as Santiago takes in her state. His beautiful sister wearing the blood of our battle and the consequence of my arrogance.

She will bear the brunt of this. Like she said a long time ago, it's always the women who pay.

Santiago's hand lands heavy on the edge of the mantel. He needs it to stand. His eyes are locked on her swollen belly.

"Santi..."

He drags his gaze to hers, and that betrayal I saw earlier is double.

"It was my fault. Not hers. I am guilty. Not her." My voice sounds strange. I never knew before today that you could hear pain.

Santiago drags his gaze to mine. I see what it costs him to do it. "You'll marry her. Today."

Mercedes shakes her head. "No, Santi—"

"You will marry her today!" he roars.

She pulls her fingers away from mine, that soft warmth gone. She takes a step toward him, and Marco, his driver and personal guard, appears in the doorway, confused momentarily at the sight that greets him, then shocked as his gaze settles on Mercedes.

"I won't marry him," Mercedes says. I see what it takes for her to steel herself. "You can't make me anymore."

It's the wrong thing to say because her brother turns his rage-darkened eyes to her. But the instant he steps toward her, I am between them, shielding her with my body.

"Get the hell out of my way," he tells me.

Marco comes into the room. I can take each of them separately. Probably not both at once, though.

"I am responsible, not her. You won't punish her."

Santiago's gaze is cold, jaw set, eyes narrowed. "She will do as I say. And so will you. You will marry her. Today."

I set my jaw too. How long have we been friends? How much have we been through together? His darkness I know. The violence that killed his father and brother. That ultimately took his mother. That claimed pieces of him. I was there for him through it all.

But my darkness? The truth that lurks inside me? He has never seen my rage, my beast. I have never allowed it. What kind of friend am I? One-sided. He doesn't know me. Doesn't know what I'm capable of. If he did, he certainly wouldn't allow me to marry his sister. He wouldn't ever have let me near her.

"Do you fucking hear me?" he demands of me.

My heart races, a fresh coat of sweat breaks out over my forehead, and I'm transported back to the punishment room, where I stand watching as my grandfather rages. As he tears into the skin of my mother's back while his beast roars, all teeth and hate and savagery. And I am paralyzed in the face of his fury.

What did I feel then? Anything? Fear? For myself or her? Fear of him. Fear that I am like him.

I can't keep Mercedes. Because keeping her will inevitably lead her to that place. To stand where my mother stood and bear the consequence of my beast. No. I have to let her go. It's the only right thing to do, yet I'm not strong enough to do it. It's why she's been here so long. Why I've kept her even though I've known all along it was only a matter of time. I need Santiago to take her away knowing what it means for our friendship, the scraps left of it.

"I can't do that," I say, my voice steady but different. Hoarse and with an edge. "But I will take responsibility for the child—"

He eats the space between us, and Mercedes sets her hand at my back when he and I stand nose to nose.

"You will not ruin her."

What can I say to that? I already have. More than he can know, I think. I feel it in the burning touch of her hand, hear it in her quiet breaths at my back. I've seen it on her face too. In her eyes. I was her first. The damage I did goes far deeper than the eye can see.

She is thoroughly and irrevocably ruined.

I have done that.

Is it any comfort that I, too, am destroyed?

I will stand with her, but I can't take her hand. I can't do what he asks of me and have her hate me more than she already does. Already should, at least. But that's the thing with Mercedes. She is so much more fragile, more tenderhearted than anyone knows.

"Judge—"

"I am sorry, Santiago. I cannot."

He looks at me like he doesn't believe me. Like he doesn't know me. And he knows I mean what I'm saying. I see it in the slight slumping of his shoulders. In the crease between his brows. As if my betrayal is slicing deeper still, and he doesn't understand why.

"Marco. Take my sister to the car."

Mercedes's hand trembles at my back, but before Marco takes a step forward, she clears her throat and walks around me. Santiago's eyes burn into me as I watch her walk away, head held high.

Marco follows her. I look at the closed door, the emptiness, the finality. But it's not time for that just yet. This isn't finished yet. And so, I turn to face my best friend. A man I love like a brother. But that's what brothers do, isn't it? Mine put a literal knife in my back. What I've done to Santiago is no different.

"Now I understand Vicarius," he says quietly.

"Do not punish her, Santiago. The fault is mine. Entirely."

"Your betrayal wounds me like nothing ever has."

I swallow the lump in my throat and try to breathe.

"I would have welcomed the union of our families. But you choose to shame my sister and, in turn, me. Your punishment will be the severing of our friendship. And you alone are responsible for it. Know that, Judge. You chose this. And may you suffer the consequence of your weakness for the rest of your life."

10

JUDGE

A gloom different from the one of the last weeks settles over the house once Mercedes is gone. The staff is quieter than before, tiptoeing around me. Santiago's curse seeps into every aspect of my existence, snuffing out any light, any air.

And I deserve it.

Over the next week, Lois packs Mercedes's things. Santiago sends a driver to pick them up. I hope for some news of her, but the driver, a stranger to me, doesn't say a word to any of us. Simply loads the van with her things and is gone.

It's in the second week that I receive word from an unlikely ally. Ivy.

She is safe. She'll be alright.

I read it three times and finally breathe a sigh of relief. I sit on the edge of her bed. It's been stripped, the room empty of any evidence of her ever having been here. I realize now that it's gone how the delicate scent of her perfume hung in the air here. I've moved her soaps and lotions into my bathroom in a strange effort to keep her close. To keep some part of her.

I consider my reply. I have questions, but it's not appropriate. I know that. I had the chance to take responsibility properly. I had many opportunities to make her mine in the correct way. And I know Santiago would have welcomed the union of our families. I have always known that. But I made a choice just as she did when she decided not to swallow that pill. And so, I type out a simple thank you, tuck the phone into my pocket, and stand.

The door opens then, and Lois peers inside. "There you are."

I look at her. She smiles her best smile. "Everything alright?"

She nods. "When the girl brought down the sheets, I found something that must have gotten mixed up in it. I thought you'd want to have it." She walks toward me as she takes an envelope out of her apron pocket. "I guess it was in her pillowcase or perhaps under the sheet."

I take the envelope, oddly grateful for the find, and I know she's looked inside from the expression on her face.

"Thank you, Lois."

"Will you take breakfast in your study again?"

"No, thank you. I'm going to head into the office early." I had cleared my calendar while my face healed enough that it wouldn't raise eyebrows. It wouldn't do for a judge to sit on the dais looking very clearly beaten.

"Alright."

"Lois," I say before leaving the room. "Has my mother been in touch?" My mother. Only one person had access and the ill intent to send that bloody sheet Santiago received in its glass and brass box.

"Nothing yet, sir. Paolo is keeping an eye on her cottage, but she seems to be away."

"Thank you."

I tuck the envelope into my breast pocket and hurry down the stairs and to my study to pick up my briefcase. I won't let myself look at the contents until I'm at the office because this strange surge of excitement must be quelled.

All evidence of that day has been cleared in my study, too, except for missing, broken furniture that will need to be replaced and the spot on my grandfather's portrait where the glass box struck. I could have it repaired, but I find I don't want to. So instead, the portrait stands against the wall wrapped in brown paper. A few days ago, I decided that I'll move it to the punishment room.

I pick up the papers I need and tuck them into my briefcase. On the desktop, I glance at Mercedes's phones. Her old one, which I keep charged and on in case Vincent Douglas texts again, and the one I'd given her. Nothing has come through on either. I leave them there and head through the house and out the front door, where Raul stands beside the Rolls Royce ready to take me into the office. He greets me as usual and opens the door. The staff knows what happened. Gossip like this is too juicy to stay quiet. But they are discreet enough.

The envelope burns a hole in my pocket throughout the drive, and as soon as I'm ensconced behind my desk, I take it out. It's unsealed, so I flip the flap open and reach inside. When I see what it contains, my breath catches.

She must have been to a doctor. I'm holding images from a sonogram. When did she do that? I see the date in the top right corner. Of course, the time she was at Madame Dubois's house. Her friends probably arranged for it.

But I don't care about that. Because what I see here makes me realize she didn't tell me everything. Probably didn't dare to and I can't blame her if I think of my behavior since I found out. I must have terrified her.

My throat goes dry as I look at image after image. There must be a dozen.

Mercedes isn't pregnant with my child. She's pregnant with my children. Twins.

A strange rush of emotion courses through me at the sight of them. I spread them out across my desk and study them in disbelief. Twins. My father had a twin. He passed away before he turned one. I can't tell if they're boys or girls or one of each, but what I'm feeling is something I've never felt before. There's a foreign undercurrent to the despair that has settled over me. An almost joy beneath it all at this scene laid out before me.

Children.

My children.

A thing I never thought I would have.

I don't know how long I sit there, but the buzzing of my phone startles me back to reality. I push the button. "Yes, Meredith?"

"Sir, someone's here to see you. He says he's your brother?"

Theron?

"He doesn't have an appointment..." she rambles on, but I don't hear it. Theron is here? I guess he got tired of waiting for me to come to him.

"Send him in."

"Right away, sir."

I collect the sonogram images just as the door opens, and I look up at Theron for the first time in the months since I found him in that hotel room with a needle in his arm. He looks good. Better than he did when he first returned to the house. He looks healthy.

He whistles as he takes in the space, and I see it through his eyes. It is spectacular with the deep chestnut leather furnishings, the tall windows, two on either side, draped with heavy, ornate curtains. A bookshelf at my back contains leather-bound volumes of law books, and my massive antique desk is set at the center of the room.

I tuck the images into their envelope and slide them into a desk drawer as I stand.

"Impressive," Theron says, entering and approaching my desk.

"What the hell are you doing here?"

"Meredith out there... it's Meredith, right? She didn't even know you had a brother. Am I your dark secret too, Judge?"

"This isn't a good time. You shouldn't be here. I'll let you know when you can return."

"Yeah, well, I think I'll be waiting until hell freezes over for you to put the welcome mat out."

"Can you not be a selfish prick for once in your life? You think you have any right to be here after what you did?"

He steps closer, his eyes searching my face. The bruises have mostly faded, but when you look close, you can see the lingering evidence of them. Not to mention I haven't slept much and probably look like shit.

"What the hell happened to you?" he asks seriously.

I study him, waiting for some taunt, some mockery, but it doesn't come.

"Judge?"

I exhale. "Nothing I didn't deserve." He's wearing dark jeans and a charcoal V-neck sweater. He pushes his hair back, but it flops forward again. It has recently been cut. And the five o'clock shadow along his jaw gives him a devious look. He looks good, though. Healthy.

And I'm fucking tired. I brush my hair back, gesture to a chair, and take a seat too. I lean an elbow on the desk and rest my chin in my hand. "Didn't I have to sign some release papers?"

He grins wide, and there's my cocky brother. He is charming. I will give him that. It's when that charm turns malicious that he's dangerous. "I worked it out. But I did wait for you. And wait. And wait. But I guess life is busy when you're Lawson Montgomery."

"Fuck you, Theron. What do you want? What will it take for you to be gone because I can't deal with you right now."

His lips move into the shape of a smile, but there's darkness behind it. "It's what everyone wants to know. How to get rid of Theron for good." He looks around the room, eyes falling on the decanter of scotch against the far wall, and stands. "You ever get tired of it?" he asks, moving toward the drink.

"Tired of what?"

"Of being yourself. What's the expression? Wherever you go, there the fuck you are." We study one another for a long moment before he shakes his head and turns his attention to the bottle of scotch. "May I?"

"A little early, don't you think?"

He shrugs a shoulder.

I gesture for him to go ahead.

"You?"

"No, thank you." I haven't had a drink since that day. I don't trust myself to stop if I start.

He pours for himself, toasts air, and drinks a sip. He stays where he is and watches me thoughtfully. "What I did to Mercedes…"

I wait.

"Hurting her like I did, scaring her." He drinks the contents of his glass and sets it down. His jaw clenches. He's steeling himself. I wait until he meets my eyes again. "I should never have hurt her, and I owe her an apology at the very least. I owe one to both of you."

This is different. Not what I expected from Theron. Him actually taking responsibility. I stop myself at that because who the fuck am I to cast stones?

"What happened to you? The last few years?" I ask.

He pours himself another and drinks a long swallow. "I found myself some trouble like I tend to do," he says dismissively.

"I paid a lot of money to some very bad men, Theron. That's not going to cut it."

He swallows the rest of his scotch and sets the glass down, then slips his hands into his pockets, and all of a sudden, he looks like he used to when we were kids. When we were friends.

"Learning I was a bastard... finding out like I did, it fucked with me. What the old man did was cruel."

"I know. But you need to get over it. He's dead and gone."

He snorts. "Get over it. Easy for you to say."

"No, Theron, it's just fucking reality. You move on, or you're stuck in the past."

"I hated you, you know that?"

"Oh, I know. And if I ever forget, I have the scar you left to remind me."

He drops his gaze, looking ashamed. The truth is, I have long understood why he did it. And I have long forgiven him.

"I blamed you for being born a Montgomery. Something you had no control over just as I had no control over my own parentage. After that night, when Mom showed me what Carlisle did to her and told me you stood by and allowed it, it was easy to hate you. Hell, without that, it would have been easy. You got everything I wanted. And I didn't even want it all. Just a small slice. The piece I thought I deserved. I was owed. I didn't feel bad blackmailing the old man. Threatening to tell everyone the dirty little secret that was me. But I guess I started hating myself a little too, you know?"

I watch him and realize this is the most honest he has ever been. The most real.

"The mob, well, that was accidental at first. I was partying. A lot. I met a woman who turned out to be the sister of one of the heads of the families in northern Italy. By then, I was pretty heavily into cocaine. And this woman had her own agenda. Stupid, I know, but as I said, I was high, and she turned my head." He looks wistful. Sad.

"Where is she now?"

"Dead." He's quiet like he's remembering. "We stole from him. It was her idea, and I helped her. And when shit hit the fan, she thought she could talk to him. They were blood. Turns out blood doesn't mean what she thought."

"Did you love her?"

He shrugs a shoulder. "I don't know. I was high all the time. At first, I was just having fun. But then things got heavy. Serious. She hated him, and when she betrayed him, he had her killed. Only let me live so that I could pay him back with interest of course.

He knew who I was by then. The family name. The money he thought I would inherit."

"A hefty sum."

"I shouldn't have let her go to him."

"You can't change the past, Theron. But you can choose your future."

He looks at me oddly as I hear my own words.

"How was Mercedes? After?"

"Pretty fucked up."

He exhales, forehead wrinkling as he takes it in. "I want to apologize to her. I need to."

"Yeah, well, she's got other things on her plate at the moment."

As if on cue, a familiar voice has us both turn toward the door. Heels click as two women hurry and argue at once—Meredith and someone I wouldn't expect to find here. Solana.

Solana comes into view first. She stops in the doorway, eyes dark with rage.

"Sir, I tried to stop her," Meredith starts, coming up behind her.

"It's fine," I tell Meredith, standing and walking around my desk. "Close the door, Meredith." Because this is going to get ugly.

"Uh... okay," Meredith manages as Solana takes me in, sees the bruises still healing on my face, and understandably, makes an assumption.

The door has barely clicked when she charges

toward me, all five feet three inches of her. "What the fuck did you do to her, you fucking bastard!"

I'm ready to catch her, but before I need to, Theron grabs her from behind, wrapping an arm under her breasts and pinning her against himself.

"Whoa, sweetheart."

"What the—?" She clearly hadn't realized anyone else was in the room, and for a moment, her attention is diverted as she struggles against Theron, who chuckles—*mistake*—and grips her wrists in one of his hands. That is until she slams the high heel of her shoe down on his foot.

"Fuck!" He releases her, and she turns to slap him.

"Solana, stop. Wait," I tell her.

She turns to me, her arm still poised to slap until her eyes roam over my face again.

"Hear me out. Please."

"Where is she? It's been a week. No call. No proof of life!"

"Proof of life?" Theron asks.

She turns to him. "Who the fuck are you?"

He smiles. "His brother." He gestures to me with a curt nod of his head.

"Figures," Solana says with a sneer, then turns to me. "Where is she, Judge? Did she do that to you?"

"No. I don't think she's capable of that."

"Oh, you don't know what Mercedes is capable of. You never have. Where is she? I can't get past the gate at the house. Neither you nor she returns my messages. Georgie's on his way to the house again, and when I tell him you're here, he'll fuck you up worse than that if you don't tell us right now."

"Jesus. Take a breath, hellraiser," Theron says.

She swivels her head in his direction. "What did you call me?"

He puts both hands up in mock surrender. I see the amusement on his face and hope for his sake she is too distracted to. "Nothing. Nothing at all."

I can't see the look she gives him, but she turns her attention back to me. "Sit down, Solana."

"Tell me where she is," she says, choosing to remain standing.

"She's at her brother's house."

She studies my face again, gaze growing concerned as she understands who did the damage. "Is she okay?"

"I think so."

"You think so?"

"She is."

"How do I get in touch with her?"

I take a piece of stationery and scroll through my phone to find Ivy's number from the text she sent me.

"Here. This is Ivy's number. She's Santiago's wife. She sent me a text to let me know Mercedes was safe. You can try calling her, but I can't promise anything. This is out of my hands, Solana."

"What do you mean you can't promise? How is it out of your hands? Don't tell me you just let her go?"

It's my turn to look away in shame, that darkness descending again. That absence of Mercedes. The knowledge of what I did.

"Jesus. You're a real prick, you know that?" She stands, snatches up the piece of paper, and walks out of my office, slamming the door behind her.

11

MERCEDES

"Mercedes." A gentle hand settles over my back, and I squeeze my eyes shut, burying my face deeper into the pillow.

I don't know how many days I've been at the manor now. I just know I can't bring myself to get out of bed. I can't stop crying. I can't let go of the pain. But most importantly, I can't forget Judge's final words echoing through my mind. His declaration that he couldn't marry me.

That simple denial haunts me, day and night. Every waking second. In my heart, I always knew it would come to this. He told me he'd never marry me, and I had prepared for it. I just didn't expect that to be the last thing he'd ever say to me. I didn't expect him to let me go so easily—as if it wasn't breaking him in half the way it was breaking me.

He's rid himself of me completely, sending my things back without a protest. Not a word. Not... anything.

"Mercedes." Antonia's soft voice comes again as she tries to stir me from my melancholy. "Please, sweetheart. You can't stay here forever. You need to eat."

A fresh wave of anguish pierces my heart because I know she's right. I can't stay here forever. I need to pull myself together and take care of my babies. But even just the thought of getting out of bed feels like too much to accomplish.

"Antonia, can you give us a moment?"

I recognize the voice from the door as Ivy's. She's been to see me every day since I've been here, unlike Santiago. At least that's one thing I can be grateful for. I don't think I could take another verbal lashing from him in my current state. And while Ivy and I have always been on tenuous ground, I have to admit it's surprised me that she hasn't come here to gloat. She could have kicked me when I was down, and I wouldn't blame her for it. But I don't think that's why she keeps showing up every day.

"Of course." Antonia gives my shoulder one last squeeze and moves from the bed. "There's food just there. Maybe you can get her to eat something."

After a few moments of silence, I hear the door shut, and Ivy comes to sit in the chair next to the bed. I feel her eyes on my face, and I wonder if she thinks I'm pathetic. The old me would have cared.

She would have sat up straight and made some bitchy remark to show her... and the world... that nothing gets Mercedes De La Rosa down. I'm realizing just how much I don't care about others' opinions anymore. That woman died somewhere between Judge's capture and my rebirth.

"I know you're hurting," Ivy says, her voice quiet but firm. "And I know you aren't the kind of woman who accepts help easily, particularly from someone like me. I think, coming to understand Santiago as I do, it's safe to say you are another De La Rosa who found a way to thrive in chaos and pain. You learned to go it alone, and that's admirable. But right now, you need to learn to accept help when it's offered to you, regardless of the source."

Her observation throws me slightly off-kilter, and I don't want to admit that she's right, but I can't deny it. Santiago and I are very much the same. We were raised with brutality and a militant structure, each of us finding our own ways to cope in such an emotionally sterile environment. Mine was never allowing anyone to see me falter. Never letting my head hang for even a second. Allowing anyone to see me vulnerable was unfathomable. Even now, it pains me to consider accepting comfort in my darkest hour. But Ivy has made it clear she knows that, and still, she has no plans to go anywhere.

"It isn't the source," I rasp, my voice hoarse from

sleeping too much. "I hold no ill will toward you anymore, Ivy. I just don't know how to do this."

She's quiet for a pause, and then she surprises me by moving to sit on the bed next to me.

"I know it's not something we can talk about easily," she says. "But I have been where you are. I have felt what you're feeling right now, and I almost let that darkness consume me. I wanted your brother's love. I wanted his warmth, and I thought I would die without it. It's the kind of pain that becomes a part of you until you think nothing can touch it. But I'm here to tell you there's one thing stronger than that pain. One thing you will come to understand."

"And what is that?" I choke out.

"Your love for your child," she murmurs softly. "That love will eclipse everything else. It will change you. There's nothing else in the world like it. No matter how broken you might feel, I can promise you, the moment you meet that baby, the world stops spinning, and you realize your true purpose in this life. You will do anything to protect them. You would gladly lay down your life for them. And I don't need a crystal ball to tell you that you'll feel the same."

"I don't know if I'll be a good mother." The confession falls from my lips unbidden. "I'm terrified I'm going to screw this up."

Ivy laughs gently. "Oh, don't worry. You will screw up. We all do. But what matters is that you keep trying. You learn from your mistakes, and you do better."

Her admission eases some of the anxiety in my chest because at least I know I'm not alone in that department.

"Now here comes the hard part," she says.

"What's that?"

"You have to start now. You need to get up. Move. Eat. Function. Even if you don't feel like it. Your baby needs you. It's time to remember who you are and show that child the De La Rosa blood runs strong. With that, you can conquer anything."

Her words settle over me, and as much as my brain wants to disregard them and stay exactly where I'm at, I know she's right. I've wallowed. I've grieved. But I have a life to create. I have a future to establish. And I can't do that lying in bed feeling sorry for myself.

"Okay," I whisper.

"Good." She reaches for my hand and squeezes it in hers. "Now first thing's first. We need to get you cleaned up."

I nod. Ivy pulls back the covers, and slowly, I sit up. It's harder than I expect because I'm weak, my muscles aching from days of doing nothing. When my feet hit the floor, and I try to stand on my own, I quickly realize that I can't.

"It's okay." Ivy grabs my arms. "Your body is tired. Let me help you."

I don't want to let her help me, mostly because I'm stubborn, and I was actually inspired by her reminder of the blood that runs in my veins. But I know she's not going to let me give up now when she's gotten me halfway.

"Remember, I've been where you are," she says. "I know it's not fun. I'm still not back to a hundred percent myself, but I have a few party tricks from my physical therapy that will make it easier."

She maneuvers herself in front of me, bends, and wraps me in a hug. Immediately, I stiffen, and she laughs.

"Yep, just like your brother. You both need to work on human affection, but I can promise you, I'll save a real hug for another time."

I realize as she starts to pull me up with her what she's doing, and surprisingly, it works. Within a moment, I'm on my feet, and Ivy has her arm wrapped around my waist in support. But that's only the first stage of the battle, and walking becomes another challenge with my legs stiff and uncooperative. It isn't until I've managed five steps that my body begins to relax slightly, and we traverse the distance into the bathroom with slow but certain progress.

Ivy leads me to the bathtub, and I grip the porcelain as my knees bump against it.

"Are you okay?" Her hand hovers near my arm as she releases me, and I nod.

"I'll be okay, thank you. You can go."

"Oh, no." She shakes her head determinedly. "That's not happening. I'm not going to leave you in here to fall."

"I won't," I say, but even as the words come out of my mouth, we can both hear the lie.

"Another De La Rosa trait," she mutters as she turns on the water. "You should know I've become a pro at managing stubbornness, so your protests are lost on me. Just remember, it wasn't that long ago the roles were reversed, and you were watching me in a similar situation."

She sets the plug into place, adjusts the water again, and then comes to stand behind me. I'm wearing an oversized T-shirt and shorts, and it isn't without difficulty that I take them off. Getting naked in front of my sister-in-law isn't on my top ten list of things I ever wanted to do, but it's either her or Antonia.

It's not until she helps me out of my shirt and discards it on the floor that I hear the quiet gasp from behind me. And then it hits me.

My scars.

I suck in a sharp breath and wait, tension blooming in my chest. It isn't as if I'd forgotten they were there, but I had become used to not hiding them with Judge, and even Lois. I wasn't thinking about Ivy seeing this part of me. Now that she has, there's no turning back.

"Mercedes." I feel her trembling hand on my shoulder, emotion choking her voice. "My god. Who did this to you?"

I dip my head, too choked up to speak myself. I'm so fucking tired of crying. I don't want to spend one more second like this. Ivy seems to understand that, and she lets me have this moment, not pushing it further as she changes tack.

"Let's get you in the tub. I'll help you wash your hair."

It isn't an easy feat, but she does get me into the tub, and almost immediately, the warm water loosens some of the stiffness in my body. I relax into it, and Ivy fingers the delicate chain around the back of my neck.

"Should we take this off first?"

"No." I shake my head, my fingers coming to rest on the necklace.

She pauses, and there's an understanding in her voice when she speaks. "It's beautiful."

I don't have to tell her who gave it to me. She knows but doesn't say anything about my desire to keep it on. I'm grateful for her compassion, and even more so that she washes my hair gently and efficiently.

It's so strange how my hatred for her clouded everything else about this woman. But now, in my clarity, I can see her for what she is. She is a gentle woman. A kind woman. She's a woman who, despite all odds, loves my brother. And I know she's a good mother too. I admire her for all those things, but most of all, I admire that she could find it in herself to forgive me and help in this way.

"Let me brush this conditioner through your hair." She walks to the vanity and grabs a comb, and I curl my knees into myself, staring at the wall.

When she comes back and starts to work the conditioner through my ends, I close my eyes and release a painful breath.

"My father."

She pauses, the words lingering between us. "Your father?"

"The scars," I explain, my voice almost too faint to hear.

Another stuttered breath leaves her lips, and slowly, she returns to her work. "I'm so sorry, Mercedes."

We leave it at that, and I don't know why, but it feels like a weight has been lifted off my shoulders. This burden I've been carrying for so long has been heavy, but even just acknowledging it helps. And in a way, it feels like the playing field has been leveled now. Ivy knows my vulnerability, just as I've known hers.

We settle into a comfortable silence as she finishes with my hair, and I use the sponge to wash my body. It's exhausting and time consuming, and it only gets harder as I exit the tub and she wraps me in a robe before drying my hair and leading me back to the bedroom.

The bed is already calling me back, but Ivy has other plans, taking me to the small table and chair and sitting me down to eat.

"Try to finish half of it," she suggests. "It will help you get some energy back."

To my surprise, a small tendril of hunger curls in my stomach when I smell the gnocchi soup. They've forced me to eat something small every day, but it's been mostly broth and smoothies. Things I could consume with little effort. Today's meal is one of my favorites that Antonia used to make me often. It takes longer to eat, but as I do, I start to feel some of the fog clearing from my head.

"Is Santi still angry?" I ask between bites.

Ivy shifts on the chair next to me, and I know that's a yes. But she tries to soften the blow. "He'll get over it. He has no choice. I think more than anything, he's hurt. He feels betrayed by Judge, and he's worried about your future."

"I'm going to be okay," I tell her, and for the first time in days, I feel it's true. There will always be a part of me that's emptier without Judge. A broken, hollow part of me that aches for him. Though I have no choice but to move forward for my children.

"I know you will," Ivy answers with a reassuring smile. "I'll be here for you, no matter what."

"Thank you." I dip my head to hide the emotion in my eyes. "That means a lot to me."

"Your friend Solana has been in contact," she informs me. "I've been giving her and Georgie progress updates."

"Oh." I set the spoon aside and stare at the remaining soup, too full to finish. "I need to contact her. I'm sure they've been worried sick."

"You can use my phone." Ivy holds it up in offer. "Anytime you want to talk to them."

I nod at her, grateful. "Maybe after dinner. I need some time to prepare."

A smile curves her lips, and she dips her head in understanding. "Okay. Tonight then. I'm going to leave you to rest, but only for an hour. And then I'm going to bring Elena in here, and we're going to do some online baby shopping and put a dent in your brother's credit card."

I laugh at the idea, but it fades away quickly as I consider the looming conversation I've yet to have with him.

Ivy hands me some books and magazines to keep me busy if I want them, and then heads for the door. But before she closes it, I stop her.

"Hey, Ivy?"

"Yeah?" She turns to look at me.

"It isn't baby, as in singular. I'm having twins."

"Oh, my god." She claps a hand over her mouth to cover her small shriek. "Twins?"

I smile too, the excitement on her face contagious. "Yep. I'm really in it now."

Her eyes brighten, and I can practically see the wheels turning in her mind as she speaks. "Okay, we have a lot to do. Names. First, we need some books for those. And then baby shower planning. Oh my god, nursery themes..." Her voice trails off as she shakes her head as if to stop herself. "You get some rest. I'll be back with books. And a notepad. Oh, and desserts!"

And just like that, she whirls from the room, leaving me there with a strange new warmth in my chest. It isn't quite happiness, but I think it's something I need more right now. I think it's relief.

The following week passes in a blur with Ivy keeping me busy. Every morning, she comes to my room with sweet Elena, allowing me to hold her and love on her while she makes plans for an upcoming baby shower... date unknown.

Neither one of us has mentioned the small hurdle that I have yet to talk to my brother, but we both know it's coming. Every day, I'm getting stronger. I'm feeling more like myself again, only a different version. My chest still aches every time I think of Judge, so I try not to think about him, although it's impossible to do at times.

At night, I talk to Georgie and Solana on the phone, and they are both just as excited as Ivy to help me prepare for the arrival of my babies. They've asked when they can visit me, but I tell them I'm not sure yet. And when I indulged my masochistic side by asking how Judge was when they saw him, I was met with a lingering silence on the line before Solana told me he looked like hell. She then proceeded to tell me she was firmly team Mercedes, as if that was a thing, and he probably deserved it. But even as she said it, I could hear the slight, unwanted pang of sympathy in her voice. I told her there didn't need to be sides on this one, and admitted that no matter what, I will always love Judge.

Those words still ring true, as hard as it may be to say them out loud. Solana didn't seem all that shocked by the confession, and with some reluctance, she agreed to bring him some more balm from her shop for his scars.

With that settled, I spend my time focusing on the more immediate future and the biggest hurdle I have yet to overcome. I know it's not going to be an easy task, but I've been preparing all week, and this morning, I asked Ivy to make the request.

I'm waiting anxiously in my room when she finally comes to meet me, and I can tell by the set of her shoulders that she's just as nervous as I am.

"He's ready for you."

I nod, rising from my chair and smoothing down my modest black dress. It's a far cry from my usual style, but I figured I better dress the part before I face my brother. Every detail will matter, and I need to prove to him that I'm not making a reckless, spur-of-the-moment suggestion.

I join Ivy at the door, and she gives my arm a reassuring squeeze before we walk down the hall in silence. It's strange being back in this house. It's the home I grew up in, but it doesn't feel like that anymore. It feels like Ivy belongs here, and I never did, and surprisingly, I'm okay with that.

"Are you sure you don't want me to go in with you?" Ivy asks as we pause outside Santi's study.

"No." I offer her a grateful smile. "This is my battle. I want him to see that I'm capable of fighting it on my own."

"I understand." She nods. "I'll wait for you upstairs."

With that, she leaves me, and I steel myself as I draw in a long breath and knock on the door.

"Come in," Santi calls from the other side.

My fingers tremble slightly on the knob, but I don't give in to the desire to hesitate before stepping inside. My brother is at his desk, waiting for me with an expression I've come to know well. It's the same expression my father wore when he was disappointed. And in some ways, that's always been difficult for me. Because I love my brother, but I am haunted by his similarities in appearance to the man who broke me down so brutally.

Santi would never physically hurt me. Not intentionally. But he unknowingly produces the same undercurrent of fear in me at times. For most of my life, I have tried to make him proud. I never wanted to let him down because I was afraid if I did, the consequences would be too severe. Yet, even as I face him presently, noting the lingering tide of anger in his features, I know one thing without a doubt. He loves me, and I love him. Regardless of everything that has happened, or what may come, that one thing is undeniable. So with that in mind, I hold my head high, and I begin.

"I know you probably expected me to come here and atone for my sins, brother. You're disappointed in me, and for that, I am sorry. But I'm not sorry for what happened. I'm not sorry that I fell in love with a man, even if he doesn't love me back. And I'm not sorry that I'll have his children and raise them on my own."

Santi shifts, his brow furrowing, but he doesn't respond, so I continue.

"Over the years, you have taken on the burden of caring for me. I know you've done it from a place of love and a desire to protect me. I have always been grateful for that. But I have long resented the hypocrisy of the rules bestowed upon me by The Society. I am a daughter of the upper echelon, and I understand that I represent the De La Rosa name with every decision I make. Regardless of those facts, you cannot tell me that I have done anything the men in IVI don't do themselves every day. I had a relationship before marriage, and perhaps it didn't work out the way you would have liked, but I don't regret the experience. Given the chance, I would do it all over again, even if it means being shamed in The Society's eyes."

Santi folds his hands across his desk, the vein in his neck pulsing. It's hard to get a read on him right now, but I don't know how long he'll let me talk, so I keep going.

"It's an unfair double standard, and we both know it. I'm not a little girl anymore, and I'm capable of making my own decisions. I understand you might see some of those decisions as mistakes, but this—" My hand settles over my belly. "I will never see as a mistake. I'm going to be a mother, and my children will only ever know love. I'll do what I must to take care of them, regardless of what you say here today. But I am asking you, as my brother, my protector, and the head of our household, to give me that opportunity without a fight. I'm not going to live here, Santi. I won't remain a prisoner any longer, allowing others to move me around like a chess piece. I have a life outside. Friends. A home. I'm capable of standing on my own, and if you release me, you will see it firsthand. I want you to be a part of my children's life, just as I want to remain a part of Elena's, but I am done playing by everyone else's rules. If you don't give me the opportunity to go freely, I will leave on my own at the first chance, and as painful as it will be, I won't come see you again."

A strained silence settles over the room as I finish, and Santi leaves the words hanging between us for so long, it unnerves me. His eyes move over my face, then he rises from his seat and walks to the window, giving me his back as he stares outside. I'm not sure what to expect from him because I've never given him an ultimatum like this. There's a chance he might see my demand as a slap in the face. There's a chance he might just try to lock me up in my room and never let me leave. History dictates it's likely to be one of those two options, but he surprises me with an admission I didn't see coming.

"Ivy told me about your scars."

My shoulders tense, and I suck in a muted breath, hoping he can't see my despair in the reflection of the window. I told myself I wasn't going to fall apart, but I didn't prepare for this. It has long been a De La Rosa tradition that we bear our shame in secret. For Santi to even mention this has knocked me off balance, and I'm not sure I can bring myself to speak.

"I wish you had told me." He shakes his head. "I would have murdered him myself."

His words stun me, not so much by the bluntness, but the anguish in his tone.

"And I will give you this, Mercedes. You are right." He turns to look at me, his eyes softer than I've ever seen them. "I've failed you."

"That wasn't what I meant, Santi," I croak. "I have never seen it that way."

"Maybe not." He shrugs. "But that's because you want to see the best in me. It doesn't change the fact that it's true. I was supposed to protect you, and clearly, I've been failing for many years, far longer than I ever knew. You didn't feel safe to come to me with this. You were just a little girl…" He swallows painfully. "And you endured it on your own. You've endured most things on your own. Yet I've never given you credit for it or tried to understand the reasons."

"We were both just doing the best we could," I answer in a whisper. "That's all we knew how to do. It's how we survived."

He dips his head, shaking it as if he can't accept that. Santi has always taken the responsibility of our family to heart, and I know it doesn't matter what I say right now. He will feel guilt for not preventing or changing my fate regardless.

"I put you in this position by doing what I thought was best for you. I've made choices that altered your life irrevocably, and whether or not you regret it, I do. Because I can see now I've caused you further pain. And I can admit that perhaps I don't know what's best for you." He stuffs his hands into his pockets, jaw set with reluctant determination. "What I want for you is simple. I can't change what's happened, but I can change how we go forward. And going forward, I want you to be happy."

I open my mouth to respond, but he shakes his head, forcing the rest of the words out even though it's obviously difficult for him.

"I know you're capable of standing on your own. You're old enough to make decisions for yourself, even if I don't necessarily agree with them. It pains me to admit that I've made great miscalculations in judgment and entrusted you with people I shouldn't."

He doesn't mention Judge by name, but it's evident by the way his eyes flare that's exactly who he's referring to. I want to defend him, tell him it wasn't Judge's fault, but Santi doesn't give me that chance.

"This is where we're at. You said you want to live a life free from the rules, but I need you to be aware of what that choice means. Without being wedded, you will be an outcast from IVI. That I cannot change for you. They will whisper. They will judge you for it, even if it is irrational. So if this is the path you choose, I must advise you that you have to be willing to let that part of your life go. You will no longer attend the events. You won't associate with your friends in The Society. You will have to accept a different life from the one you have always known. But in doing so, there is one assurance I can give you, and that is regardless of you severing those ties, there is one that can't be broken. You are a De La Rosa. You are my family, my blood, and nothing will ever stand in the way of that. Do you understand?"

"I understand." I blink through my glassy eyes. "That's all I care about, Santi. If I can still see you and Ivy and Elena, I know everything else will be okay."

He nods, clears his throat, and then speaks firmly. "I'm signing over your trust to you. You have my blessing to make a life for yourself outside. However, there is one point I won't negotiate on. For my own peace of mind, I need to know you're safe, so you will have two guards watching over you until this situation with Vincent Douglas is resolved. Do you accept these terms?"

I can't help it. Despite my promises to myself that I wouldn't cry, moisture gathers at the edges of my eyes. And much to my brother's discomfort, I don't give him my answer verbally. I take the first difficult step, closing the distance between us and pulling him into a forced hug. His arms hang awkwardly at his sides until he slowly wraps them around me.

"Thank you, Santi." I burrow my face into his chest and cry in relief. "Thank you."

12

JUDGE

I sit in my car and watch the condo. It's a little after eleven at night. Two IVI guards lurk not so discreetly in a Rolls Royce, getting looks from every other resident of the small development. I understand why Santiago doesn't have more discreet men here. Vincent Douglas is still a threat. He wants to be sure if Douglas wants to try to get at Mercedes, he'll have to get past these two first.

At least with them around, I blend.

Or so I think until I hear a tapping at the passenger side window and turn to find Solana standing there, the hood of her wool cloak pulled over her head to shield herself from the drizzle.

When I don't move to open the window right away, she gives me a look and points at the button that would lower it. I push it so it comes about a third of the way down.

"Yes?"

"You are scaring the neighbors."

"No, that'd be the two soldiers in the Rolls." I point as if anyone could miss them.

"You're not exactly incognito here. Please tell me you realize that."

"What do you want, Solana?"

She reaches into her giant bag and retrieves a jar. "Here. Your salve. You're probably running low if you're using it as I instructed."

I open the window a little wider and reach out and take it because I don't think she'll go away until I do.

"Madame Dubois told me you'd be here, so I brought it with me."

"Madame Dubois is a crackpot."

"She's the real deal, Judge. And she told me a few things about you."

"Like what?" Why am I playing along?

"That's for me to know and you to find out." She pulls her arm out, straightens, and looks up at the sky. "I'd better get inside. Mercedes is expecting us." She gives me a grin just as Georgie pulls up, honking his hello to her as he parks directly in front of my car, just tapping his bumper to mine. He smiles at Solana, then glares pointedly at me and mouths an *oops*.

"For fuck's sake." I roll up my window and watch Solana slide her arm into Georgie's. They walk together to Mercedes's front door. He's carrying an enormous bouquet of roses in every color but red and some sort of sparkling beverage, which I hope he realizes Mercedes won't be drinking.

They ring the doorbell, and in the light over the front door, I see Mercedes when she greets them. When her eyes flit to me, my heart skips. But she is quick to look away, and her smile is for her friends. Not me.

I guess I'm not so incognito, not that I thought I was. Her hair is braided in one long, dark plait over her shoulder, and she has a turquoise shawl draped over her shoulders. I can't see her swollen stomach because Georgie and Solana are standing in the way, and I find I want to. I want to see it more than anything else.

I set the jar of salve on the empty seat beside mine. Solana was right. I am almost out. And the stuff is good. That lashing will leave scars but less. She delivered the first jar to my office about a week after she busted in, telling me she only did it as a favor to Mercedes because in her opinion, which I didn't care to hear but she shared nonetheless, I didn't deserve it.

A few minutes later, I see the three of them gather around the kitchen table I remember from the last time I was there. Mercedes sets the flowers Georgie brought in a vase in the center, then moves to the window, where I swear she takes a pointed moment to look at me before swiftly shutting the blinds.

I glance away, disappointed. Although I have no right to be. This is what I wanted. I chose this. I let her walk away, and I am a prick for it, just like her friend said. But I remind myself that it's better for her. Safer. I start the engine and back out of my spot, tempted to plow right through Georgie's car and give it more than a little nudge. I know what that is. Jealousy. Not like before, like when I thought he might have something with Mercedes. Jealousy that I'm not a part of whatever is going on in there. Jealous that I am on the outside. Knowing I will always be on the outside.

Santiago's curse floats to mind. I wonder if he knows how powerful words are. How I am suffering every day for the loss of her. The loss of him.

I swallow down my emotions and drive for hours, going nowhere, barely aware of what I'm doing until, closer to one in the morning, I arrive home to a quiet, sullen house. I don't sleep much anymore. I'm on autopilot. I work. I eat what I need to get through the days. And at the end of each day, I spend my evenings parked outside Mercedes's house, keeping vigil. I tell myself it's to watch for Douglas, to make sure she's safe, but I know better. I miss her. I feel the loss of her like a hole in my chest. Something I have never experienced before. And, strangely, I cling to it. I don't numb it with drink because when I'm alone and especially in the small hours of the night, I want it to wash over me. To drown me. Because at least then, in some pathetic way, I am close to her.

Theron greets me from where he's sitting by the fire in the living room with a tumbler of scotch at his side. He is in the dark apart from the small reading lamp beside the chair.

"You're stalking her again?" he asks, closing his book.

"You're here again?"

"Where should I go?"

"Somewhere else."

"Well, unlike you, I don't have multiple properties to choose from."

"I gave you the South Cottage. Go there."

He shrugs a shoulder. "It's boring." He gets up and goes to the bar to refill his glass. "Drink?"

I shake my head but don't leave. The truth is, it helps having him here. A distraction.

"Can you at least not brood. Let's go to the Cat House," he suggests.

I raise my eyebrows. "We're not friends, you and I."

He lifts his chin, expression serious. "No, I know that. You tolerate me. You will never forgive me for the things I've done."

"Oh for fuck's sake. *You* are free to go to the Cat House. Maybe it'll do you good."

"Having my brother be able to stand in the same room as me would do me good."

I ignore him. It's selfish, I know. He's trying. But I can't deal with him right now. "Although I didn't think the Cat House was where your interests lay any longer." Because ever since his meeting with Solana, he's been asking questions. "I saw Solana tonight," I taunt.

"Did you?" He drinks. "Did she ask about me?"

"No, oddly. I don't think you're as memorable as you like to think of yourself."

"Well, I'll pay her a visit at the shop."

I grow serious. "No, you will not."

"Why not, big brother?"

"You know why. If Mercedes sees you—"

"I'm not going into hiding, Judge. I told you I want to talk to her. I want to apologize."

"I don't care what you want. You'll upset her. She's in a fragile state."

He raises his eyebrows. "I'm not sure she has a fragile state."

I stalk toward him, take him by the collar, and shake him so hard that the scotch splashes from the rim of the glass onto his hand. "You will stay away from her. From anywhere she might be, or God help me—" I stop myself. God help me what? Christ. I'm even using my grandfather's words. His threats. I release my brother, pat down his shirt, and step away, raking a hand through my hair.

"I'm not scared of you, Judge. Give it up. You're not him. Besides, he'd never have wasted good scotch." He rinses his hand at the sink, then repours and drinks. "I will stay away from Mercedes to keep from upsetting her, not because you're threatening me. But I'll only do it if you have a drink with me."

"That's blackmail."

He shrugs.

"Fine," I acquiesce. He pours, and I take the glass, keeping my eyes on him as I swallow it all down.

"That's the spirit, I guess," he says, clearly disappointed. He's alone too. I know this. But I can't deal with that right now.

"There." I hand him the glass and go to my study where I'll spend the next few hours. Lois has left a note propped up against the stack of mail that dinner is in the kitchen and instructions how to warm it up, but I throw it away. I'm not hungry. I sit down and go through the letters, mostly unimportant, until I come up to a box without a return label. It only has my name on it, Lawson Montgomery, but no address. It must have been hand-delivered. Using the letter opener, I cut the tape away. It's stuffed with tissue paper, and my heartbeat quickens as I push it away because I swear I smell the subtle but distinct scent of her. Mercedes's signature perfume made just for her. And I inhale deeply, that ache in my chest throbbing. Alive. But when I see the box within the box, it's like having a knife slice through the muscle there. A sharp, smooth blade that slides easily into the tender, beating mass of it.

Because inside is the necklace. One of the few gifts I gave her. The one that meant more than I realized at the time. I take the box out, search the tissue paper for more, a note, something she wrote me. Anything. But I find nothing. Perhaps inside the rich velvet jeweler's box. I take the lid off, open the folded layers that protect the diamonds, and the throbbing in my chest quiets. Because it's just the necklace returned to me. No note. No need. Its absence speaks volumes.

I push back from the desk and take the bottle of scotch because maybe tonight I need the numbing. I pour myself a generous glass and drink it all down as I stand at a safe distance from the glinting diamond in the open box. I remember what she said when I gave it to her. That it wasn't a gift because she'd earned it. More than earned it.

I pour a second glass.

How can the recent past become so distant so quickly? How can things change so fast they leave you unable to breathe? Unable to believe they really happened to you. Because Mercedes having been here, touching her, feeling her beside me, beneath me. Being inside her. Smelling her hair. Watching her sleep. Holding her. It's as though it never happened. Or like it happened to someone else.

How can she be gone so completely, all evidence of her erased from my house? How could I have let Santiago take her away from me?

I drink three more glasses as the drizzle that had begun just a little while ago turns to an angry rain lashing the windows. It's then I snatch the necklace out of its box and shove it into my pocket. I stalk back out of the house to my car, and I drive back to her house, where the IVI guards are still sitting in their goddamned Rolls Royce watching her door like two hulking machines.

When I climb out of my vehicle, one of them opens his door but must recognize me and nods. He gets back into his car. I guess Santiago didn't give them a shoot-to-kill picture of me. I leave the car parked half in the street, half in a spot because honestly, I probably shouldn't have driven tonight. I stalk up to her door. I have a key, but I ring the bell. Well, I more lay my weight against the damn thing until a light turns on, and I see her in the narrow, rectangular window beside the door. When she sees me, she comes to an abrupt stop. I'm fucking getting soaked as lightning electrifies the sky, so I lean against the doorbell again before she finally opens the door, and we stand face-to-face for the first time since that terrible day I lost everything.

13

JUDGE

Mercedes's eyes move over me, a small line forming between her eyebrows at what she sees.

"What do you want?" she asks, tone cold. She blocks the entrance, glancing over my shoulder at her personal bodyguards.

"In," I say when she looks at me.

"Why?"

Thunder crashes, and lightning charges the sky. "It's fucking pouring, Mercedes."

"Then maybe you should have brought an umbrella. Or better yet, maybe you shouldn't have come at all." She starts to close the door, but I stop it with the toe of my shoe.

"Really? You expected me not to come after this?" I pull the necklace out of my pocket and wave it in front of her face.

"All I have to do is raise one finger, and those two will be on you before you can—"

I wrap one arm around her waist so it looks to the guards like I'm hugging her and move her back into the house, then close the door.

"Jesus!" She pushes me off, and we both look down at her nightie, an emerald-green silk gown that is soaked at her chest. Water drips off my head, my clothes sticking to me. I didn't put on a jacket in my haste. "What the hell, Judge?"

"This was a gift," I say, backing her into the wall when she tries to get around me.

"I don't want your gift. Just like I don't want you stalking me every night. Take a fucking hint." She pivots around me, but I grab her arm and pull her back.

"You will wear it. Every fucking day."

"News flash," she says, tugging free. "I don't belong to you!"

I block her with my body as I secure the necklace around her neck.

"What are you doing? Are you drunk? Jesus? I can smell the liquor!"

Again, she tries to slip past me, but this time, I take hold of her jaw, fingers digging into soft skin. I make her look at me, and in this dim light at this insane hour, I search her face, memorize her dark eyes, the scattering of gold specks. I smell her smell, that familiar mix of amber, citrus, and warm spices that I've missed too much. And I kiss her. I hold her in place, and I kiss her even as her hands come to my chest to push me away, even as she doesn't kiss me back and groans her protest against my lips instead.

I don't care. I can't. I need this too much. I need her.

"Mercedes." I kiss her jaw, her throat, the curve of her neck as I undo my belt, unzip my slacks, the need too great to wait. When I straighten to look at her, her eyes have gone impossibly dark. They glisten as her hands curl around my shoulders, and I reach under the nightie to tug her panties aside. Lifting her, I brace her against the wall, her belly firm and foreign between us.

She wraps her legs around my middle as I take myself out, and she gasps when I thrust into her, making a sound that comes from my gut through my chest, my heart, and out of my mouth.

"I need this so fucking much," I manage, kissing her as she holds on to me, grunting with the force of the fucking. I'm not sure if she's kissing me back. All I know is that I'm inside her again. Back where I belong. And as I move faster, she closes her eyes and bares her throat. When I feel her come, all I can do is watch her face. Nothing could drag my gaze away. Not those guards, not her brother, not a fucking army.

"Lawson." I'm not sure if I imagine her saying my

name or not. It's a breath, barely a sound obscured by a loud crash of thunder.

She dips her head, forehead coming to the curve of my shoulder. She's wetter now, the aftershocks of her orgasm taunting my cock, and I don't last long. I weave my fingers into the hair at the back of her skull and make her look at me. I kiss her as I come, watching her black eyes as the world stops spinning on its axis. And for an impossible moment, I am home. I am home.

I WAKE TO UNFAMILIAR LIGHT. UNFAMILIAR SOUNDS. I open my eyes to look out of a window that's not mine into a bright morning. Last night comes back to me in painful increments as the door opens, and I turn over to find Mercedes there. She stops when our eyes meet. She's wearing that silk nightie with thick, fuzzy socks and carrying two mugs of coffee. She studies me but doesn't offer a smile as she comes to the bed and holds one of the mugs out to me.

I sit up, my head throbbing, and lean against the headboard before taking the mug.

"Decaf. Sorry."

"It's perfect. Thank you."

"Aspirin?" she asks.

I sip and shake my head although even that hurts.

She settles beside me, pulls her knees into her chest, and blows on her coffee. Across the room, I see my clothes draped over a radiator to dry and try to remember when I undressed. Hell, I can't even remember how I got here. But I do remember one thing, and as I turn to take in her profile and see the necklace still around her neck, I remember fucking her in the entryway.

"You probably shouldn't have driven last night," she says as if I didn't know. She turns to look at me.

I sip the coffee. "You're probably right." I can't move my eyes off her and she seems strangely shy as I take in her belly. She's about six months now. A little more. Above her nightie, I see the swell of her breasts. They're filling up for the baby. Babies.

I finish the coffee and set the mug aside. She's still sipping hers. "Two little monsters," I say.

She looks hesitantly toward me and nods.

"Was I such a beast that you were too afraid to tell me?"

She shifts her gaze to her coffee and sets it aside. "All I knew was I couldn't terminate the pregnancy." She looks at me squarely to finish. "And I wasn't sure you wouldn't make me."

I rake my hand through my hair. Honestly, I don't know either. Would I have forced that decision on her? I'd like to think not. But more and more, I'm realizing that I don't know myself. Not really. I've been so busy trying not to be someone that I don't know who I am. Don't know which part is me and which part is me trying not to be him. My grandfather. "I'm sorry for how I was with you. I'm sorry for all of it."

Her eyes mist. She picks up her coffee as a distraction, and sips, then sets it back down. When she turns back to me again, those eyes have turned angry.

"Are you sorry for the babies then?" she spits and swings her legs off the bed.

I catch her, hold on to her because if I let go, I'm afraid she's just going to slip right through my fingers.

"Lois found the sonogram images. You'd hidden them, understandably. When I first saw them, what I felt was..." I pause, searching for the right words. "What I felt was hope. Joy maybe. Just the faintest suggestion of it."

She smiles a real smile, one that's unsure, but it, too, is hopeful. A tear slips from her eye, and I brush it away with my thumb, then slide my hand around the back of her neck to draw her to me and kiss her. She doesn't fight me. She kisses me back, and I feel more wet tears smear from her face to mine. I taste the salt of them as our kiss deepens. I've missed her so much. Jesus. So fucking much.

I draw away, and she's flushed, eyes that shiny

black they get when she's aroused. I pull her nightie off and lay her down. Strip off her panties. And I look at her for a long, long time. See how her body is changing and even more beautiful for it with her swollen breasts and protruding belly. I kiss her mouth, the space on her throat between her collarbones, her chest, and her breasts. I kiss her belly and lick the dark line that leads to her sex, where I open her legs and taste her as she moans. I note the subtle difference in her scent—pregnancy hormones, I guess—and I dip my tongue inside her, then return to her swollen clit.

She sounds the same when she comes. She grips my hair and pulls me to her, thighs closing on either side of my head, squeezing as she moans my name. When her body goes limp, I climb on top of her and make slow love to her. And I can't stop kissing her. I can't stop.

It's when we're lying in bed afterward that I see something I've never seen before. Mercedes giggling. It's such a foreign sight that I find myself staring. Then I see why. And I watch in awe as her stomach moves.

"They're kicking. Probably hungry," she says, looking at me. When I don't move, she takes my hand and lays it over her bump, and I feel it. I feel the pressing of a hand or a foot. Contact. The babies are making contact.

Mercedes watches me, but I am mute.

"Is the great Lawson Montgomery finally dumbstruck?"

"I've been dumbstruck for a long time now, little monster." I have no idea why I say it, and clearly, she is taken aback and confused.

The baby stops moving then, and I clear my throat. Mercedes looks away first, slips her nightie on, and climbs out of bed.

"I need breakfast," she says and hurries from the room.

I sit there for a minute, wondering what the fuck just happened. What I just admitted. Wonder what I'm doing.

I get up to pull on yesterday's clothes, stiff from drying on the radiator. I pick up my phone from on top of the dresser where she must have set it, and I see several notifications but ignore them. They can wait. I wash my face and work my fingers through my hair.

She's in the kitchen scrambling eggs and toasting bread when I get there. I set our mugs on the counter and pour us more coffee while I watch her, this strange, new Mercedes standing at the stove scrambling what looks to be a dozen eggs.

"I didn't realize you knew how to cook."

"It's eggs." She rolls her eyes. "But there's a lot you don't know about me, Judge. You've never bothered."

"That's neither true nor fair."

"Isn't it?"

The toaster pops.

"Can you put more bread in?"

I take the two pieces out and put two more in.

"There's juice in the fridge."

The dynamic between us is strange. Different. Domestic. But off. I remind myself that Mercedes and I do better when we fight, but I find I don't want to fight. Not now.

So I set the juice and the toast on the small table, and when the eggs are ready, I take the frying pan from her to serve us.

"Sit down," I tell her.

"I can do it."

"I know you can. I just want to. Please let me."

She agrees but only after a long minute, and I wonder if we can ever get back on the right track. What that track is. I wonder if she can forgive me because I have made mistakes with her. I applied the rules of The Society to us, to our lives at home, and I forgot that she's human. That we're both human. And that humans feel and have their hearts broken far too easily. And only when they're broken do we realize how hard it is to put the pieces back together again.

"The doors and the locks, was that you?" she asks as we eat.

I nod. I had them upgraded. "Your house was too easy to break into."

Vincent Douglas. We're both thinking it, but neither of us says it.

"How are things between you and your brother?" I ask.

"Okay, actually. We're doing well. Ivy and I, too. She's a little crazy when it comes to shopping for the babies." She smiles, and I'm glad to see it, glad to hear this.

My phone dings with a message, and I remember all those notifications but ignore it. "I will take care of you. All of you, you know that, right?"

She tilts her head, eyes scrutinizing me. "What makes you think we need taking care of?"

"I'm their father."

She shakes her head. "You don't have to do anything. You don't even have to acknowledge them. I don't need your money. I don't need your name. I don't need anything from you." I'm not sure if she intends that to cut, but it does. It cuts deep. "Besides..." She sets her fork down, her face closing off, that woman upstairs who was giggling vanished. "I know it would be difficult, what with you being the next councilor of The Tribunal and—"

"I don't give a fuck about The Tribunal."

She shrugs one shoulder, gets up, and takes her still full plate to the sink. I follow her, standing behind her as she wipes off the dish.

"Stop," I say. She elbows me so I take her wrist. "Stop, Mercedes. Talk to me."

"What do you want?" she asks, not looking at me.

I don't answer. I'm not sure how.

She turns to face me. "What do you want, Judge? Why did you come? To give me a necklace?" She reaches to unclasp it, but I stop her.

"You keep it on. Always."

"Why? What the hell does it mean?"

"The house is quiet without you. Lonely without you."

She snorts. "You can't have me back halfway. I won't settle for that."

"I'm not asking for that."

"Then what are you asking for?"

My mother's words repeat in my head. The terror in her eyes when I turned the table over.

"I feel sorry for the woman you'll marry one day. You are just like him, Judge. Exactly him."

My phone pings. Mercedes shoves to get free, but I keep my hands on either side of the counter, trapping her.

"You'd better get that," she says.

"Mercedes, you know why I can't marry—"

"You know what, Judge? I'm not asking you to fucking marry me. It's arrogant of you to think I am. But I'm also not okay to be your booty call on a rainy night when you're drunk."

"You're not—"

"That's what the women at the Cat House are for. For the Sovereign Sons to use as they please. So do me a favor. Stop coming here. Stop watching me. And just stay out of my life so I can get on with it, okay? You think you can set your selfish needs aside for one fucking minute and do that one thing for me? Or is it too much to ask?"

Her eyes are wet by the time she's done, and my goddamn cell phone starts fucking ringing now. I reach to mute it, and she shoves me away, slipping past to the hallway.

"Come back here, Mercedes." I go after her.

"Go home, Judge," she says, opening the door.

I slam it shut and take her arms. "I don't want any woman at the Cat House. I want you. You."

"Has it ever occurred to you that maybe *I* don't want *you*?"

14

MERCEDES

"Ouch." Solana bustles through my door, glancing over her shoulder at the parking lot where I'm certain she ran across Judge. "What happened there?"

"Nothing I want to talk about." I turn and busy myself with the dishes so she can't see my face. I'm haunted by what I saw in Judge's eyes when I delivered that blow.

Maybe I don't want you...

The truth and the lie are so gnarled between those words that I'm not even sure of it myself. Because I do want Judge. I know I always will. But I'm not going to accept scraps. Not for myself, and certainly not for my children.

"Hey, are you okay?" Solana presses her fingers into my back, not forcing me to look at her, for which I'm grateful.

"I don't know. I feel so stupid for letting myself get sucked back into his orbit every time he looks at me. How am I supposed to move on when he's literally sitting outside of my house every night? Hot one minute, cold the next. I can't deal with it anymore. He doesn't want me, but he doesn't want to let me go either."

Solana's silence is uncharacteristic, and when I do finally turn to look at her, she's gnawing on her lip.

"What?" I sigh. "Why are you looking at me like that?"

"I don't know," she says cautiously. "I just hate seeing you like this. You both look so… miserable."

At this, my spine straightens, and I shake my head in denial. "Well, I'm not. It's just frustrating. I didn't negotiate my freedom to spend my days playing a mental tennis match about what Judge is going to do next. I'm trying to establish a life here, and that's exactly what I'm going to do."

Solana wisely chooses not to comment further and instead takes over dish duty while I go get ready. Step one in forgetting about my broken heart is staying busy, and we've got a full schedule ahead of us today.

After I tear through half my closet, only to settle on a pair of leggings and an oversized T-shirt, we head to the birthing class. Georgie joins us for the occasion, then promptly becomes traumatized ten minutes into it, and opts to wait outside instead. Of course, it doesn't hurt that the IVI guard he's had his eye on is there to keep him company.

Once we're finished with class, we hit the mall and several children's stores to grab some baby furniture, which Georgie has promised to help me assemble. I purchase a new phone while we're out too, transferring my old number to it, and effectively cutting Judge off from that line of communication he controlled.

When that's finished, we meet Ivy for lunch and finalize our plans for the baby shower, which will be next month. She's thrown herself into the project, and I'm grateful for it, but I can't help feeling it's really not necessary for her to go to so much trouble. The only people who'll be showing up for it are my small group of friends and possibly Santiago if he cares to join. Regardless, it's something positive to focus on, and I'm happy to see that Ivy gets along well with Solana and Georgie too.

By the time we get back to the condo, I'm too tired to cook anything, so I order us pizza while Georgie somehow commandeers his crush, aka Drew the IVI guard, to help him assemble the cribs.

"He's got a talent for that." Solana watches in amusement from the kitchen as they sort through the pieces on the floor, Georgie pretending he has a clue what he's doing.

"He can smooth talk his way into anything." I roll my eyes.

Solana brings a piece of red licorice to her lips, chomps on it, and nods. "So what do you think the chances are Georgie will have that guard out of his black cargo pants by the end of the night?"

I snort. "I would say pretty good with the way they keep eyeing each other. But it won't go over too red-hot with Santiago if it happens while the guard's on duty."

"Makes sense." Solana sighs, her eyes drifting somewhere distant. "Although it would be nice if one of us was getting laid."

I feel my face flush at the reminder of Judge fucking me in my entryway last night, but I figure it's probably best not to bring that up.

"I'm sure you could find plenty of willing volunteers." I turn my attention to her.

She shrugs. "I guess. But they're all boring. I need a challenge. Someone who can handle me, you know?"

I laugh and shake my head absently as my phone chimes with a message. My stomach drops when I see that it's from Judge.

You transferred your phone number?

Why it should surprise me that he's aware of this already, I don't know. Regardless, I decide it's best not to answer.

"Hey." Solana's voice brings me back to the

present, and when I look up at her, she's chewing on the end of her licorice in thought. "What's up with Judge's brother?"

I feel the color drain from my face as I study her. "Theron?"

She pauses her chewing, clearly concerned. "What is it?"

"He's an asshole," I declare, a little too emphatically. "Why do you ask?"

"Is that supposed to be a surprise?" She arches a brow in question. "I'm guessing it's a family trait."

"It's not the same." I shake my head and force down a gulp of water from my glass. "Theron is a wolf in sheep's clothing."

"How so?" Solana presses.

Her curiosity about him concerns me. I know she met him briefly at Judge's office, and she's mentioned several times she thought he was an asshole herself. Yet there's a glint in her eyes right now that I need to quash. I never intended to tell her what happened in that punishment room, but she needs to get him out of her thoughts before she goes any further down that rabbit hole.

"He's got issues," I say. "Addiction, for starters. I'm not really sure, but there's something dark in him. I just know you can't trust him. He seems lovely and charming at first. That is until he's high out of his mind, restraining you to a bench so he can whip your ass."

"Oh, my god." Her eyes widen in shock, but I can see I've only sparked her curiosity more.

"It wasn't that kind of whipping," I clip out. "Nothing was sexy about it, and I didn't want it. I didn't ask for it."

"Oh." She frowns, swallows, and shakes her head. "God, babe, I'm so sorry. I didn't realize. Why didn't you tell me?"

"I figure there's only so much fucked up you can take at a time."

"The world you live in is different," she mutters. "That's for sure. But you don't have to handle me with kid gloves. I'm here to listen, always."

I feel better having told her, and I hope I got through to her, but something is still lingering in her thoughts. It makes me nervous because I don't want Solana getting twisted up in the warped world of IVI, especially with someone like Theron. But there's one thing I know about her. She's strong-willed, intelligent, and feisty... yet she has another side. A darker side. She's made that remark more than once about wanting a man who can handle her. Translation... she likes the dominant type. Someone who will be the alpha and try to put her in her place. That's what she meant about a challenge. And from what I'm gathering, she's sensed those qualities in Theron. I just hope she doesn't cross his path again because I doubt I'll be able to stop her from wanting a taste, even if he's not good for her.

My phone chimes again, and I consider ignoring it because I'm certain it's Judge. But Solana isn't helping to divert me by her own distracted thoughts, so I check it. And I'm surprised to see it's the last person I'd expect. Clifton Phillips. It's strange, considering I haven't heard from him since the night of that insane dinner at Judge's house. Yet here he is, texting me like no time has passed, asking if he can take me out. I reply with a polite thank you and decline the offer. But that doesn't seem to deter him because he's texting me again a moment later.

Please, let me make it up to you. That last date was a disaster.

I stare at the screen in confusion at his persistence. I don't know why the sudden interest now. Surely, after that trainwreck, he'd cut his losses and run.

"Who is that?" Solana leans over my shoulder to peek at the text.

"He's a Sovereign Son," I explain. "I think I really stuck my foot in it with him because I had a lapse in judgment and clearly wasn't thinking things through when I considered the idea of marrying him just to escape my captivity. Now, it seems he's still holding on to that hope."

"Creepy." Solana shivers. "Tell him hell no."

I laugh but decide to ignore him too. I already told him no once, and that should be enough.

"We're done!" Georgie proclaims proudly from the living room.

Solana and I both go to inspect their handiwork, which, as it turns out, isn't bad at all. When I test the sturdiness of the crib by trying to wiggle the frame, it doesn't move. A credit I silently give to Drew, the hulking IVI guard with a perpetually stern look on his face.

"Thank you." I offer them a warm smile. "This is amazing."

Drew's phone rings, interrupting the moment, and almost at the same time, the doorbell chimes. He answers his phone as I move to check the door, and then his hand catches my wrist and stops me.

"Wait here, Ms. De La Rosa." The order is barked with such authority that it really does halt me in my tracks.

Georgie and Solana exchange a glance, and then we all watch as Drew goes to the door, quietly talking into his phone to the other guard outside. When he opens the door, there's a small box sitting on the step, and a strange shudder crawls down my spine as I realize this wouldn't be from Judge. There's no way he'd not deliver something personally, and Drew confirms it when he bends down, carefully lifting the flap of the cardboard. His spine goes rigid, and he hangs up his phone abruptly, glancing at me over his shoulder.

"What is it?" I demand.

His lips flatten like he doesn't want to answer. "I should talk to Santiago first—"

"Tell me." I glare at him. "Right now, or I'll come look myself."

The crease between his brows intensifies, and he shakes his head, muttering his quiet response.

"It's a plastic baby doll, chopped into pieces... and a blank invitation for a funeral."

"I REALLY DON'T LIKE THIS, MERCEDES." SANTI'S JAW clenches as he glances around the space, searching for invisible threats. "It would be better if you came back to the manor."

I can see how difficult it is for him to make this request, rather than demanding it like he's used to. So I offer him a small smile, trying my best to sound calm.

"It will be okay. Georgie and Solana are going to stay with me. I can't let Vincent dictate how I'm going to live my life. That was the whole point of me coming here. And clearly, The Tribunal has no plans to deal with him, so this situation isn't going away."

Santi shakes his head in frustration at the observation. He's not happy with it, but it's the truth.

"Besides, I have the guards," I point out.

"And you'll have more," he grits out. "I'm calling in two additional. They'll be here shortly."

I bite back the urge to tell him that's overkill. As much as I really dislike having these random guys following me everywhere I go, I know it's necessary. And, truth be told, it does make me feel safer.

"Thank you, Santi."

He lingers, his eyes moving to Georgie and Solana on the sofa, and then back to me. "Are you sure you don't want to come home?"

"This is my home," I croak even though that's not exactly true. There's only one place that feels like home now, and it isn't here or the manor.

Santiago looks distraught by the idea, as if he's only just now realizing that he's losing me. When he sent me away, I'm sure it was in his mind that I'd be back eventually. But now things have changed permanently without any real time to accept it.

"I just want you to be safe," he says.

"I will," I assure him. "I'll be extra careful."

"And you'll call me if you need anything," he adds.

"Of course."

He nods reluctantly. Then there's a knock on the door, and everybody tenses. Only, I know before Santi even moves who it is. There is only one person who can knock like that.

"Santi." I capture my brother's arm, and he pauses to look at me. "Tell him I'm asleep."

His brow furrows, but he nods, and I move around to hide behind the door when Santi cracks it open. There's a moment of tense silence, and then Judge's acknowledgment of my brother's presence.

"Santiago."

"Judge."

More silence. Then a sigh.

"Is everything okay?" Judge grits out. "The guards seem to be on high alert."

"Everything's under control," Santi answers vaguely.

I already know without looking at him that Judge won't like this.

"Where is she?"

"Asleep."

"Why are you here in the middle of the night?" Judge asks.

"Why are you?" Santi replies.

I swallow, waiting for this to be over. The terrible part is, I want to see him. I want to open the door and invite him in and curl up in the shelter of his arms. More than anything, that's what I want. But Judge can't be my safety net anymore. I can't fall back into that trap.

"Her phone number was transferred," Judge says quietly. "I wanted to make sure she was alright. She hasn't answered my texts."

"Maybe that's because she doesn't want to," Santi snaps.

I feel the pain of that verbal blow, and I have to press my fingers to my lips to stop myself from telling him that's not true. This is what addicts are supposed to do, right? Cut off their drug of choice cold turkey? I understand now why it's so hard. I want him. I crave him. At times, I feel like I might die without him. In his warmth, nothing can touch me. Everything is okay for those fleeting moments. But then I remember the pain when he leaves me cold. And I know in my soul, for the sake of my heart, this is what I have to do.

"I know you're angry with me, Santiago," Judge continues. "But we want the same things for her. I want her to be safe. I want her to be happy."

"You have a funny way of showing it."

"I set up an account for her." He shuffles around, reaching for something before I hear him hand it to Santiago. "This is for her to take care of anything she needs. She and the babies."

"You can't buy yourself out of this," Santi growls.

"That's not what this is."

"Then what is it? Why the hell are you here, Judge?" my brother demands. "To torment her? Haven't you done enough?"

I close my eyes, wishing this would end. I don't want them to come to blows again. I can't deal with that. Not now.

"Judge." Solana joins my brother at the door, glancing around his shoulder while she secretly squeezes my hand in hers. "Just go home, okay? Tonight isn't the night to do this."

Her voice holds an unexpected amount of sympathy, and I can only imagine Judge must look a wreck if that's the case. Solana seems to be conveying something to him, and I wonder just how much he's tried to talk to her.

There's another quiet sigh from the outside, and then the sound of his retreating footsteps. I should be relieved when Santi closes the door and hands me the paper Judge gave him, but when I stare down at the account information, it burns. Right along with Santi's words. *You can't buy yourself out of this.*

I wish I knew if that's what he was trying to do.

15

MERCEDES

The next few days pass in a weird blur of dissociation. Solana and Georgie stay true to their word, sleeping over at my place while the guards outside keep watch. There are four of them now, just as Santi promised. And when I'm not at home, I spend my days at Solana's shop hanging out with her and Madame Dubois while Georgie often joins us for lunch.

Ivy has been texting me, but Santiago won't let her come to the shop with the current threat looming over my head. He's been extra careful with her since he almost lost her, and I don't blame him. In a way, it's actually kind of sweet, and Ivy doesn't seem to mind. So we make plans to meet at the manor for lunch next week.

In the meantime, I'm fielding texts from both Judge and Clifton, who has oddly only grown more persistent. My approach to both is the same, although ignoring them doesn't seem to be working. And while Judge's texts make me homesick for a place I'm not even certain exists, Clifton is getting on my nerves.

"All I'm saying is he's not buying what I'm selling." Solana drags me back to the present conversation as she straightens the inventory on the shelves.

"You don't have to text him back," I answer absently, though I am curious to know what Judge has been asking her now that he's texting her too.

"He's worried about you." She stops, tosses me a glance over her shoulder, and shrugs.

"He's so worried he tried to throw money at the problem to fix it." I glare down at the sprigs of lavender I've been trying to arrange neatly in their buckets.

"I don't think that's how he meant it."

My eyes snap up to her back, and Solana seems to sense my irritation as she turns and offers me an innocent smile.

"What happened to being team Mercedes?"

"I still am." She presses a hand to her heart. "One thousand percent. But I can still be team Mercedes and feel a little bad for the guy, can't I?"

"What would you have me do, Solana?" I grumble. "Let him toy with me for the rest of eternity, coming and going as he pleases? Using me whenever he sees fit?"

"No," she answers carefully. "And I don't think that's what he's doing. At least not intentionally. He's like a caveman. He's trying to figure this situation out with the only tools in his arsenal, which seems to be a lot of grunting and swinging his club around. In other words, I don't think he knows how to navigate his emotions."

"This sounds more and more like team Judge by the second." I wipe my hands and start to return the buckets to the display case.

"All I'm saying is anyone can see he's crazy about you, babe. But clearly, he's terrified by the idea at the same time. Something inside him is holding him back, and it has nothing to do with you."

I swallow, turning to gather another bucket so she can't see the pain in my eyes. "I can't change that. Believe me, I've tried. If he wanted to let me in, he would. But in case you haven't noticed, I'm having not one but two babies soon. My focus has to be on them, not someone who can't decide if he wants to be in our lives."

Solana wisely chooses not to answer, and I'm glad for it. If she knew how many doubts I already had every second of every day about what I'm doing, she would probably pounce on the chance to bring us back together.

We continue our work in silence, her stocking the shelves while I adjust the displays. It's ten minutes to closing when the bells on the door ring, and a familiar voice infiltrates my thoughts.

"Mercedes?"

I turn to see Clifton standing there, and I stare at him in confusion. "What are you doing here?"

His eyes move over my round belly before darting back to my face, a cool smile curving his lips. "I hope you don't mind. I haven't been able to get in touch with you, so I asked your guards. They told me you've been spending your days here."

"This is... unexpected," I say. In other words, it's fucking weird.

Clifton seems to be oblivious to my discomfort, or if he notices, he doesn't care. "Look, I heard about your... situation." He nods to my belly. "Whispers are going around. One of the guards let it slip. But not too many people know yet. I think we can still salvage this."

"Um... what?" I blink, and then blink again, clearly confused.

"I put the word out that I was courting you," Clifton explains as if this is totally rational. "Back before the dinner at Judge's house. We can still save your reputation. I have a priest from IVI who's willing to marry us for a fee, and he'll add whatever date we want to the official paperwork. We can just tell everyone we wanted to enjoy our honeymoon period before we made it public."

I stare at him in stunned silence. What he's

offering might have seemed chivalrous at one point in my life, but I'm not stupid. Clifton isn't here out of the kindness of his heart. He wouldn't chain himself to me and go through all the effort to save my reputation because of his undying love. We barely know each other, but what I do know is clear.

"And you'll get what out of this exactly?" I arch a brow at him.

He shifts, acting affronted for about two seconds, then shrugs. "Half your trust."

"I see."

The words settle between us, and he stares at me expectantly. And truth be told, if I wanted to save my reputation in The Society, what he's offering me is a good deal. We could marry, live as roommates, and I could raise my babies with the full protection of IVI behind me, minus the shame. There's only one glaring problem with that plan.

The space on my neck was reserved for one man's crest, and it sure as hell isn't his. And I know now with certainty, even if Judge doesn't want to marry me, I can't marry anyone else. Because he's already tattooed his name across my heart. I won't pretend otherwise.

"Thank you, Clifton." I side-eye Solana, noting she's listening to our conversation with an amused gleam in her eyes. "What you're offering me is generous, all things considered. And I'm grateful. But truthfully? I'd rather be ruined in the eyes of The

Society than marry someone I don't love. So respectfully, I can't accept your hand."

For a moment, he looks so shocked by my refusal that he can't seem to speak. Then there's a brief flash of disappointment and, finally, a renewed determination.

"You're hormonal." He holds up his hand when I glare at him. "You have a lot on your plate. Just consider it. I don't need an answer today."

Before I can give him that answer without mincing words this time, he leaves. Just as soon as he does, Solana promptly bursts into a fit of laughter.

"It's like a scene straight from a historical romance," she chokes out. "Oh god, you have to admit it was a little funny."

"So funny." I roll my eyes as she wipes the tears from hers. "Now, if you're done laughing at my suitors, can we go home?"

"Yes." She nods, forcing her lips into a smile. "Let's get out of here before any other dashing young fellows come calling for your hand."

16

JUDGE

My cell phone, which is sitting on my desk, pings with a text from Paolo.

She's here, and the car is ready.

My mind is a flurry of activity, of possibilities and what-ifs as I leave the office and drive home. There's just one thing that lingers beneath the surface that I am trying hard not to think about. Mercedes's last words to me that morning at the condo.

Maybe I don't want you...

Every time I replay that moment, it's like a piece of my heart is carved out. I have fucked up so completely. How could I be such an idiot? I can't even blame her. She's right. I am arrogant. What I want, I take. And she doesn't deserve the scraps I am capable of giving.

But am I capable of more?

No. I knock that thought out before it has a

chance to root. Absolutely not. I need to hear her now. I have been selfish, and I need to put her first.

And then there are the babies to consider. The thought that I won't be a part of their lives is a reality I can neither understand nor accept. But accept it, I must. I have to let her get on with her life.

But what the fuck does that even mean? She'll marry someone else? Let them bed her? Let them be a father to my children?

The thought sends a wave of raw fury through me.

I pull up to the front of the house, where Paolo has the Range Rover ready for me. It's the car the dogs fit into. I walk into the house to find a flurry of activity, a sight I've not seen in too long. Lois and several of the staff are gathered around the little puppy who is putting on a show as they ooh and aah over her, petting her, and taking turns cuddling her. Even Pestilence is nudging the little Doberman with his nose, wanting to play.

"Judge," Lois says, looking up at me from her crouched position. "She is too sweet by far!"

I have to admit, she is charming as she comes over to sniff my shoes, Pestilence settling at my side as I bend to pet her, turning her face up to mine to get a look at her.

"Does she have a name yet?" One of the girls asks.

I lift the puppy and straighten. "Not yet." I'll

leave that to Mercedes. "Is the car loaded?" I ask Paolo.

"Yes. Mercedes will have enough supplies for a week, and I'll drop by with more then."

"Thank you," I say and whistle for Pestilence to follow. Outside, I open the back of the Range Rover, and Pestilence jumps in. I set the puppy down beside him and watch Pestilence nudge her backward as I close the hatch.

Right now, given what's happening with Vincent Douglas, I'd like nothing more than to drag Mercedes back to the house and lock her in my room to keep her safe. Well, Douglas is one of the reasons. This puppy is my effort at giving her the space she is asking for. But I'm not above a little emotional blackmail to get Mercedes back here of her own free will. I'll take what I can get, any scraps she'll offer me.

How the tables have turned, I think, as I climb into the driver's seat and head to the condo.

When I arrive, I'm glad I don't see Solana's or Georgie's cars in the lot. Two Rolls Royces are parked side by side, watching Mercedes's house. I open the hatch of the Range Rover, and Pestilence jumps out. The puppy tries to follow suit but hesitates at the high drop, whining. She sits and looks up at me, her little tail wagging.

Oh, yes. Blackmail.

I pick her up, nod a greeting to the guards, and

head to Mercedes's front door. Pestilence sniffs everything in the front garden before coming to stand by my side as I ring the bell and wait for her to open the door.

Her steps falter when she sees me through the window but then Pestilence barks, his tail wagging as he sees her, and she hurries to open the door. She doesn't greet me, doesn't even smile, and before she can say a word about the puppy in my arms, Pestilence is nudging his nose against her, demanding all her attention.

"Hey you," she says in a warm tone she uses with the dogs. She crouches down and lets him lick her face as she pets him. "What are you doing here?"

I clear my throat and invite myself in.

"Oh," she says, tone cooler as she looks up at me. She straightens.

"They can't drive themselves," I say.

"Hm." Her gaze moves to the puppy, whining to be free of me, and she smiles wide. "Who are you?" Mercedes takes her from me. The puppy instantly loves her, her little butt wagging along with her tail as she licks Mercedes's face while Pestilence demands more attention.

"Do you like her?" I ask. Closing the door, I get a look at her belly in the T-shirt she's wearing. It's clearly not a maternity shirt because it hugs her tight, leaving a strip of skin exposed above her leggings. It takes all I have not to reach out and touch her stomach, lay my hand over my babies inside, wondering if they'll recognize my voice, my touch.

When I meet her eyes, she's watching me. "What is this, Judge?"

I raise my eyebrows, suddenly uncertain of my plan. "You don't like her?"

"No, it's not that. I love her." She says the words so easily, so honestly. Have I ever been so easy with those particular words? Never. "But what are you doing?"

"Well, I thought it was time to get a new puppy. Keeps the boys on their toes."

It's her turn to raise her eyebrows. "Really? Because four giant Dobermans aren't enough?"

I clear my throat. She sees right through me. "She's for you, actually. I thought since you love the boys so much, you could have your own. The condo is too small for four grown dogs, obviously, but one, perhaps... I thought..." She isn't going to make this easy. "Paolo will train her, don't worry. She'll stay with me until she's fully housebroken. But I thought Pestilence could stay with you in the meantime."

Her eyes narrow. "So she's for me?"

I nod. "If you want her."

"Like a gift?"

I notice she's not wearing the necklace, but I bite back my comment. "Yes."

"What's her name?"

"She's not yet named. You can choose."

"Oh." She looks at the small puppy as she sets her down. "Okay. I think I'll call her Kali."

"Kali?"

She grins at me. "Like the goddess who devours her enemies."

"Oh. Alrighty then. Kali it is." I am confused. But okay.

"And you want Pestilence to stay with me?"

"Can I come into the house?" I ask. She hesitates. "Just for a few minutes. I'm not going to do anything, Mercedes. I am just here for the dogs."

"Mm-hmm, sure." She folds her arms across her chest and gestures to the living room with a nod of her head. I see a candle burning on the mantel, and the scent of cinnamon wafts through the air. The sun is fading in the early evening hours, and there's an overall warmth in the space. A coziness.

Steam rises from a mug of tea on the coffee table, and on the floor is a laundry basket full of baby clothes that she's been folding. The sight of it hits me hard.

This is happening.

We are having babies.

We.

No, not we.

She.

"Mercedes, I—"

"You want something to drink?"

I drag my gaze from that stack to her. I shake my head. "Let me go get Pestilence's things." I need to get out of here for a minute.

"You haven't asked me if he can stay. You just assume like you always do."

I push my hand through my hair, my eyes falling on those clothes again. I drag a breath in. "You're right. I'm sorry. I thought you'd want that. I thought—"

"I'm not scared of Vincent Douglas, Judge. He can't touch us. I won't let him."

"He's a man, Mercedes. If he gets to you, he will do what he wants."

"Like most men."

"He means you harm," I say, cataloging the blow but not allowing myself to waver right now. Her safety is why I'm here. "And a man will always be able to overpower a woman. If he gets in here—"

"Have you seen the guards my brother has posted outside?"

"If he gets inside..." I ignore her. "They can't help you. Not if they don't know. I prefer you to come to the house of course," I start, putting it out there. She scoffs at the idea. "But I won't drag you there against your will."

"Wow, that's a change for you. Does it hurt to consider what someone else wants?"

I grit my teeth. "It's safer for you if Pestilence stays. He won't let anything happen to you."

As if sensing the tension, Pestilence comes to nudge Mercedes to pet him. "He can stay. I'd love for him to stay. But not because I'm scared."

I nod. "That's all I want. I have his things outside. Food, a bed, everything he needs. Paolo will replenish his supplies. You just call me if you need anything. Anything at all. I can come to walk him—"

"I'm sure I can handle walking him."

"Of course. Let me go get his things." I walk out of the house, noticing the shopping bag of diapers by the stairs. One of the guards helps me unload Pestilence's supplies.

"Where would you like him to sleep?" I ask Mercedes when we're alone again.

"With me."

I nod, and without waiting for an invitation, I carry his bed and the bag of infant's diapers that are already sitting by the steps up the staircase. She follows and directs me where to put his bed. I then stand facing her, the bag of diapers in my hand, completely at a loss for what to do but unwilling to leave.

"Those go in the nursery."

I follow her down the hall to the room freshly painted in shades of the softest green and yellow, stickers of colorful animals on all the walls, two cribs set at opposite ends, a changing table, and boxes and boxes of unpacked things for the babies.

She watches me as I take it in.

"You can put the bag down, Judge."

I turn to her and nod. "Where do you want the diapers?"

"I'll do it."

"Please. Let me."

She points at the cupboard under the changing table, and I get on my knees to unpack the impossibly small diapers. I stack them along with the baby wipes, then stand back up.

"Do you need anything?" I ask.

"We're fine. We have everything we could need," she says, hand on her belly. I want to ask if they're moving. If I can touch them. But I know I can't.

"Oh." I reach into my pocket and take out the envelope there. I hold it out to her.

She takes it and looks inside.

"The sonogram images. I kept one. I hope you don't mind." She eyes me, and for a moment, I wonder if she'll want me to give it to her. But then the puppy barks downstairs, and we both turn to the door. Mercedes is the first to leave the room. I take one more look around, feeling lonelier than I have ever felt, and follow her back downstairs and out to the patio. She opens the little gate and lets Pestilence and the puppy down on the grassy area where the puppy relieves herself.

"Your brother increased the guards." He doesn't know I have eyes on Douglas. I should communicate it with him.

"It's fine, Judge. Santi is handling it."

"Why? What happened?"

"It's handled." She turns to walk away, but I grab her arm to stop her. She looks down at where I'm holding her, but I don't let go.

"What happened? Because something did."

"Nothing."

"Something. What was it?"

"I received a package the other day. Delivered to my front door."

My blood turns to ice. "What package?"

Her expression falters, and I glimpse the thing she's trying to hide. Fear. "Mercedes? What package?"

She doesn't quite look at me when she answers. "A chopped-up baby doll and a blank invitation to a funeral."

"What? Why didn't I know about this?"

"Judge—"

"Jesus Christ. I was here. I asked him."

"Judge, you're hurting me."

I look down at where I still hold her and see how I'm squeezing. "Shit. I'm sorry." I loosen my grip but don't let go. "Come home with me. Please. I can protect you."

She closes her eyes and shakes her head. "This is my home, Judge." Are her words forced, or am I imagining it?

"No, it's not. Let me protect you."

"My brother—"

"Please, Mercedes. Let me take you home."

"You need to go. I want you to go."

I stare at her, not wanting to hear her. She pries my fingers from her arm and turns her back to me to call for the dogs.

"I will keep Pestilence. But you need to respect my decision and go. Now."

"Don't shut me out."

She drops her head. "Please, Judge."

"At least—"

She spins and slaps her hands against my chest. "Just go. Fucking go! Just this once, put yourself second and do what I ask for a fucking change!"

Tears wet the skin around her eyes, and I see the effort this is costing her. See how my being here is hurting her. I watch her for a long minute, letting the look in her eyes burn itself into my brain, the pain inside them like a brand on my skin.

I nod. Because I can't speak. And when the puppy comes strolling up the stairs, I scoop her up and walk through the house and out the front door.

17

JUDGE

I call Ezra as I drive to Santiago's house. "He delivered a fucking package to her doorstep!"

"Judge, calm down."

"How did he do that, Ezra?"

"Have you checked your messages?"

"What messages?" I ask, digging my phone out of my pocket, which I'd muted due to a full day of hearings.

"The three I left you a few hours ago."

I see the notifications on my screen.

"He slipped the guards. Must have gotten out overnight."

"Are you fucking kidding me?"

"I'm sorry, Judge. I've let both men go, and we're scouring the city for him. He won't get near her."

"He delivered a fucking package to her doorstep! I'd say he got near her!"

He mutters a curse on the other end, and I force a deep breath in as I near the gates of De La Rosa Manor.

"He's not done with this. With her," I say.

"No, you're right. But we'll find him."

"I need to go. Let me know as soon as you know anything."

"I will. I am sorry, Judge."

I know he can't control everything but fuck, this? I disconnect the call and look into the security camera outside the gates of the manor. I'm not sure Santiago will let me in, but I'm unwilling to leave until he sees me. But then, without a word through the intercom, the gates begin to open, and I drive to the entrance where, before I even come to a stop, I see my once best friend standing, arms folded across his chest, mouth in a thin line, his face closed to me.

But I don't care about that. I can't. Not right now.

I bring the Range Rover to an abrupt halt, and I am out of the driver's seat the moment I jerk it into park.

"You didn't think I needed to know about the death threat at her door?" I stalk to him. I haven't even closed the car door.

He straightens, gaze cool. "No, I didn't think it was any of your business."

"Are you fucking kidding me?" I shove him backward. "She receives a death threat, and you don't think it's my fucking business?"

He gets in my face. "No. I didn't think it was. And how do you know anyway? Did you go near her again?"

I clench my jaw and raise my chin.

"For fuck's sake. She doesn't want to see you. Get it through your thick head." He looks me over from head to toe. "You look like hell. Go home and get some sleep. There's nothing for you here." He turns to walk back inside.

"Yeah well, she's carrying my children, so get that through yours!"

He spins on me, the same rage from the day he learned about us burning like a brand on his face.

"Santi?" Ivy comes running out and catches his arm.

He stops and snarls. But gets himself under control. "I'm very aware of what you did to her, Judge," he says, hands fists at his side.

"We need to talk."

Ivy looks from him to me and back.

"No, we don't. I said all I needed to say to you." For a moment, I think he's going to walk away, but then we all turn at the whine that comes from inside the Range Rover.

"Shit."

"What is that?" Ivy asks, smiling when Kali pops her head up to the window.

"I need to let her out. Can you watch her? I need to talk to your husband."

"I said…" Santiago starts, but Ivy squeezes his arm.

"I'll watch her. What's her name?" she asks as I open the hatch for her to scoop Kali up.

"Kali."

"Oh," she says, clearly confused.

"Mercedes named her."

"Ah." She stifles a smile and clears her throat to set Kali down. "You two go ahead. Kali and I will play."

I look at Santiago, who only turns to walk into the house. I follow him through to his study, where he sits in his chair behind his massive desk. I close the door and remain standing.

"He was at her house?"

He only studies me with narrowed eyes.

"Look, we want the same thing. Mercedes safe. Mercedes happy. Right now, the first part of that is crucial. You're going to need to work with me, or so help me, I will drag her back to my house and—"

"I should let you because that would sever any lingering emotions she confusedly feels for you."

That makes me pause. Because what Mercedes said was not this. But haven't I said the opposite of what I want, too? To protect her. Protect myself. Because there is something that I've managed to avoid for a very long time. All my life, in fact. I have never had a real relationship. I can count on one hand the dates I've taken women on. I go to the Cat

Their Reign 163

House. I fuck. I leave. I am not blind to the pattern. And I understand why. It's hard not to.

I am afraid.

And now I'm afraid not only of hurting her. Perhaps the true fear is entirely out of my control.

I know I'm not worthy of her affection or her love. But if she did give it to me and then took it away, what would become of me then? If what's happening to me now is any indication, it does not bode well for me.

"I don't understand, Judge," Santiago finally says, drawing me out of wherever the hell I was going.

I sit.

"What don't you understand?"

"Why won't you do it? Marry her? You have feelings for her that's obvious. I see it on your face even now. And she has feelings for you. So why don't you just fucking do it and put everyone out of their misery?"

I bow my head. Can I tell him? Can I reveal this terrible secret to him?

"You know me, Judge. You know everything about me. Yet you don't talk about your past. Never have. Or on those few occasions it comes up, it's very superficial. Perhaps you think I haven't noticed, but I have, all these years. I know I don't see you, not all of you. So what is so fucking dark that you're willing to lose everything, every goddamn thing, to hide it?"

I swallow over the lump in my throat, feeling

sweat collect under my arms and along my forehead. I look at my friend, but I'm looking through him.

He snorts, shaking his head. He gets up, pours a scotch, and sets it on the desk in front of me.

"Does it have anything to do with the tattoo on your back? The one I never knew you had."

I pick up the scotch, barely controlling the tremble of my hand. I drink a swallow.

"Or the scar it hides beneath? The knife wound."

I swallow the contents of the glass. He doesn't pour another. Just sits back and watches me. This is too hard. It's not that I want to keep my secrets. It's that it's too hard to share them. To bare myself like that.

"You will miss out on a family. Is that what you want?"

I look at the ring on my finger. All Sovereign Sons wear them. The Montgomery insignia, law and consequence. I can almost hear Carlisle.

"You know Hildebrand is salivating to have me on The Tribunal."

"I know."

"He and my grandfather had been planning for it for years." I make myself look at him. "Hildebrand thinks we'll make a powerful team."

Santiago watches me. He doesn't speak, and I can't read him. But I don't expect him to make this easy for me. Why would he? If our roles were reversed, I'm not sure I'd even give him this chance.

And perhaps a few years ago, he wouldn't have. This is Ivy's doing. She has softened him.

"He sees something inside me that he recognizes, Santiago. A violence..." I trail off because I don't know what else to say.

"Is it there?"

I nod once.

"Have you unleashed it on my sister?"

"No."

"Did you force her?"

"She was in my care. I was the one in control."

"Did you force yourself on her against her will?"

"No. Christ. I am not that beast."

His expression softens infinitesimally. "I know that already. I just wasn't sure you did."

That surprises me, and I find I'm struck mute.

"A neighbor delivered the package. Douglas is smarter than to come to the house with the presence of the IVI guard. But he is determined." He opens a drawer, takes a box out, and sets it on the desk.

I stand, open it, and look inside to find the baby doll chopped to pieces and the funeral invitation. My blood turns cold just like it did when she described the contents. "Christ. Did she see this?"

"No, the guard wouldn't let her."

"Let me take her home." He raises an eyebrow, and I know it's at the word home. I press on. "I can keep her safe. He won't have access to her in my house."

"Nor would he in mine. But she doesn't want that, and I think it's past time we respect her decisions for a change."

"This is life or death, Santiago."

Standing, he comes to put a hand on my shoulder. "Imprisoning her in your house or mine is a different sort of death. And neither you nor I want that for her."

18

JUDGE

I'm on my way home when my phone chimes with a text. At a traffic light, I check it. It's Solana sending some idiotic message I don't understand.

Solana: *Dun dun da dun...*
Me: *Can you forget my number?*
Solana: *I hear wedding bells.*
Me: *What?*
Solana: *Didn't you hear? A certain eligible Sovereign Son has asked for Mercedes's hand in marriage. He was very romantic about it too...*

When I pull a U-turn in the middle of the intersection, cars honk their horns, sending traffic screeching around me. My cell phone drops to the floor as I press the gas pedal and race to the apothecary. I double park outside, fuming as I stalk into the shop. Solana is with a customer, and that crack

Madame Dubois is filing her nails from her table, wearing a sly smile on her face.

"I'll be right with you," Solana says with a shit-eating grin. "Why don't you look at our selection of mood-enhancing elixirs over there."

I grit my teeth and consider shaking her when I hear Kali bark. Shit. I forgot about her, and I don't need her pissing in my car.

"I will be right back!" I tell Solana and go back outside, the bell over the door irritating now. Opening the hatch, I lift Kali out. I should put her down in case she needs to piss, but instead, I grin and walk back inside the shop, forcing myself to smile at the customer leaving with her purchase, then set Kali down.

"Aw!" Solana's face breaks into the biggest smile as she comes rushing to the puppy. "Oh my goodness, aren't you the cutest thing ever! Georgie is going to love you!" She picks the puppy up, hugs her tight, and Kali licks her face, and it fucking pisses me off.

"What was your text about?"

She straightens, holding on to Kali. "Judge, you do not strike me as a puppy-loving kind of guy honestly. Don't take that the wrong way."

Does she hear the rattle in my chest? If so, she clearly has a poor sense of danger. Because she just smiles wider.

"What the fuck did you mean?"

"Let me take the puppy outside. I think she needs to use the facilities," Madame Dubois says, slinking over to take the dog. These people are going to fucking kill me.

"You should get some sleep, Judge. You really look like hell," Solana says once we're alone and she's moved behind the counter to put some things away in the display case. "I do have something for that."

I inhale deeply. "You are testing me."

"What?"

"What. Was. Your. Fucking. Text. About?"

She shrugs her shoulders. "What I said. I thought it was pretty self-explanatory."

I grip the counter and count to ten. "Do a better job of explaining."

"Clifton Phillips is an old flame of hers, am I right?"

"Clifton fucking Phillips? A flame? I don't think so."

"I mean, he's cute, I guess," she wavers. "If you like that type. Although I guess you worked the brooding, domineering asshole type out of her system."

"When did you meet him? Was he invited to one of your little events the three of you have?"

There's that grin again. "No, I met him here. He tracked Mercedes down. Romantic, am I right?"

I feel my brain rattle against my skull.

"And then he proposed to her! Right here in my shop!" She sighs with a big smile on her face, but something is off.

"He did what?"

"It was something to see, that's for sure."

Madame Dubois returns, and Kali's nails click on the floor as she returns not to me but to Solana.

"What did she say?"

Solana picks Kali up and cocks her head at me. "You don't look happy for her, Judge."

"What did she say?"

"I'd think you would welcome a proposal from a Sovereign Son. I mean, you're the big shots, right? The upper echelon of your creepy little Society?"

"Solana. I am going to ask you one more time. What did she say?"

"She's thinking about it. But I'm guessing we may be hearing wedding bells soon. I'd get on that if I were you, Judge."

The bell over the door rings as if taunting me, and I turn to find Georgie walking in. He gives me his usual glower for a greeting, then beams to Kali. I don't wait for him to even get to her, though, before I snatch her from Solana's arms, to the protest of both dog and woman, and stalk out of the shop thinking of how exactly I'm going to kill Clifton Phillips.

19

MERCEDES

"Soooo?" Solana's stare burns a hole into the side of my face as we sit on the sofa watching a trashy reality TV show. I think the entire premise is that everyone just gets drunk every night and makes bad decisions, but I'm not entirely certain.

"So what?" I toss a piece of popcorn into my mouth and chew on it.

"Nothing to report today?"

I turn to her, arching an eyebrow in question. She's been acting strange since she got here. Almost like she's expecting something, but I don't know what.

"Will you just tell me what's on your mind?" I groan. "Clearly, there's something."

"It's nothing." She shrugs a shoulder innocently. Too innocent if you ask me.

"It's something," I mutter.

Pestilence settles into my side, laying his head over my lap while he eyes the popcorn bowl.

"You're in a mood." Solana plucks a piece of popcorn from the bowl and feeds it to the dog. "Did something happen with Judge today?"

"You mean other than him trying to lure me back to his house with a puppy?" I remark dryly.

"I think it's kind of cute." Solana scratches Pestilence's head and wiggles her brows. "I wouldn't mind a hot guy trying to lure me back to his place with a puppy."

I toss her a glare. "Did you just call Judge hot?"

Another innocent smile. "Why, does that bother you? He is hot. I have eyeballs. Can't I just make that casual observation?"

I drag my annoyed gaze back to the TV and pretend to watch the cast fight about who slept with who last night. Solana knows she's getting under my skin, and she's doing it intentionally. But the question is why.

"It must be something in that Montgomery blood," she adds thoughtfully. "Theron might be an asshole, but he's got that dark, brooding thing going for him too."

"Solana." I start to protest, irritated that I haven't squashed this fascination of hers like I thought I did. But before I can even get into it, a thunderous knock rattles my door.

"Whoa." Solana's eyes widen as she looks from me to the door. "Who could that be?"

"I have a feeling…" I drag myself up off the couch and walk over to the entryway, staring through the peephole to find the last two people on earth I expected to see on my doorstep tonight.

I fling open the door, wondering if I'm losing my mind as my eyes roam over a bloodied Clifton. Standing beside him, holding him up by the collar is Judge, and he's sporting a blood-spattered shirt himself.

"What in the fresh hell—"

"Tell her," Judge demands, practically shaking Clifton like a rag doll in his grasp.

Clifton's gaze moves to mine, terror swallowing the light from his eyes. "I retract my offer!"

I hear Solana's snort from behind me, and suddenly, everything starts to fall into place. She must have told Judge about this. It's the only thing that makes sense.

"Clifton—" I start, but he cuts me off, shaking his head vigorously.

"I retract my offer! I won't marry you. I don't want you!"

"Gee, thanks." I roll my eyes before turning my attention to Judge. "Are you satisfied now?"

He releases Clifton with a grunt and shoves him away. "I'll be satisfied when I cut out his fucking eyeballs if he ever looks at you again."

Clifton heeds his warning by scurrying across the lawn, running as fast as his legs can carry him before he trips and falls face-first into the grass. It doesn't escape my notice as he drags himself back up that his clothes are torn. Judge has really done a number on him. He'll probably take weeks to recover. Judge, on the other hand, only has some bruising around his knuckles to show for it.

"Was that really necessary?" I ask him.

"Obviously, he didn't get the fucking message the first time. So yeah, it was."

Judge is still fuming, his eyes burning as they roam over me possessively. I feel that look right between my thighs, and I'm sure he sees it.

"What are you doing here, Judge?" I choke out. "I—"

He grabs me by the waist and pulls me into the house with him. "What I should have done a long fucking time ago."

Solana clears her throat behind us, alerting him to her presence, and Judge shoots her a glare as if this is all her fault somehow.

"I think I'll just..." Solana gestures to the door as she heads for it in a hurry.

"Yeah, you do that," Judge growls at her.

The moment she's gone, he turns his fiery gaze on me, wraps his fingers around the nape of my neck, and tugs me against the hard plane of his chest.

"Over my dead body." His lips brush against mine, the heat of his words singeing me. "Will I ever fucking let you marry him."

Before I can tell him I wasn't planning on it, his mouth covers mine, and a fire ignites in my belly as his rough hands lay claim to my body. He grabs my ass, squeezes, and groans before he yanks down my leggings, forcing them off me. At the same time, I'm tugging his shirt free from his trousers, pulling buttons free from holes, then reaching for his zipper. He hoists me up into his arms, my belly bumping against his as he carries me up the stairs. As we go, clothing follows in our wake. I don't even know how we're managing it, but our hands are everywhere. Tugging hair, touching skin, branding heat into our bodies.

"Judge," I whimper as he releases my mouth from his only to drag his teeth down my neck.

"Goddammit, Mercedes," he growls. "This belongs to me. All of it. Every fucking part of you. Do you get that?"

I make no protests about that as he spreads me across the bed and kicks off the pants around his ankles. Then he's on me. His body presses me down, his warmth soaking into my skin, his scent all around me.

"Judge," I beg again.

He kisses me, spreads my thighs and drags his

cock through my arousal. I'm beyond ready for him even though it's only been a matter of minutes.

"Say it." He brands my face with his fingers, torturing me as his cock throbs against me. "Tell me who this belongs to."

"You." The word leaves my lips unbidden, and if that wasn't bad enough, I emphasize it. "Only you."

His groan of approval drowns out everything else, and then he thrusts inside me, his fingers digging into my hips. His mouth coming back to mine. Our teeth clash, tongues invading, and I let him fuck me like it's our last day on earth because I fucking need it.

I arch into him, and he gives me all of himself. Every thrust. Every fierce sound that leaves his lips. His agony is a match only to mine, which he eases when he makes me come, not once, but twice around him.

The spasms are still ricocheting through my body when he unleashes with a painful growl, releasing himself inside me with one word so full of finality, it breaks me.

"Mine."

He buries his face into my neck, inhaling me as his hands move over the curve of my belly. And I can't help it. My chest heaves as painful emotions erupt from me with a sob.

Judge freezes, pulling back to look at me with terror in his eyes. "Mercedes?"

"Why do you keep doing this to me?" I cry. "Why can't you just let me go?"

He pulls away from me, and I feel the loss of his warmth, the loss of our connection as he hauls himself to the edge of the bed and averts his gaze. His head hangs heavy, his back muscles rippling with tension as he drags a hand through his hair.

"I can't." His choked response invokes a renewed combination of anger and heartache.

"Why?" I demand. "Why, Lawson? Fucking tell me."

"Because goddammit." He turns to look at me, eyes filled with a fire he's never let me see. "I fucking love you, Mercedes. Can't you understand that?"

Those words tear through my armor, lodge deep in my heart, and fragment as I release another quiet sob. This one is something else entirely.

"You love me?"

"Yes," he rumbles. "I fucking love you. I have loved you… longer than you could ever know. You're carrying my babies. I'm inside you. And I can't let you go. I won't apologize for it. If you want Clifton, that's too goddamn bad because it's not happening—"

"Then why?" I cut him off.

His eyes move over my face, searching. "Why what?"

"Why won't you let yourself have me?"

He turns away then, shielding his emotions

while he processes them. When he does finally respond, his voice is so brittle, it's barely audible.

"Because the thought of losing you for good fucking paralyzes me. And if I fuck it up, when I fuck it up, I know I won't survive that loss."

His words stun me into silence, and at the same time, they confuse me. All this time, this is what he's been afraid of? He's keeping me away to protect himself from something he's already doing to himself? To both of us.

"You've already pushed me away," I tell him. "How is that any different?"

His head dips in defeat. "It's not. I thought it would be if I was controlling when or how it happened, but it's not any different. You're too good to be real. It's impossible to allow myself to think, even for a second, that I could actually have something like this. But I can't let you go either. I've tried. Fuck, I have tried."

I sit up and move to him slowly, terrified he might flee at any moment. But he doesn't. Even when he feels my hands wrap around him from behind, my lips pressing against a scar on his naked back. A scar he bore for me.

"Lawson?"

He shivers beneath my touch, and I grab his face, turning him to look at me. His eyes are soft and vulnerable in a way I've never seen, and I know something has shifted. This isn't a fleeting glance.

He's giving me the key, unlocking himself, and he's letting me in.

"I love you too," I whisper.

He shudders, pain twisting his features, and it's only then I understand why this is so hard for him. All this time, I couldn't make sense of it, but it was staring me in the face. He told me about his family. The betrayal he felt from his brother. The coldness I've seen in his mother when she looks at him. The agony he feels over letting her down. Everyone he's ever loved has let him down and made him feel unworthy. Why would he think I'd be any different?

That realization wrenches my heart, twisting me up inside as I squeeze him in my grasp, trying to convey the intensity I feel for him.

"I love you," I tell him again. "And I always will. No matter how much you piss me off. No matter how much we fight. Regardless of what the future brings, you are imprinted on me. Do you understand that? You are and always will be the one person who makes me feel this way." I crawl onto his lap, bringing his fingers to the beating pulse of my racing heart. "That song is just for you, Lawson Montgomery. Nobody else gets that."

He cups the back of my skull in his palm, drags me to him, and kisses me. It's a kiss of possession. Of claiming. But something deeper. Something unbreakable. And that tether that binds us will always be. I know it. He knows it. And we give in to it, for real this time.

He sets me on his cock, back where I belong, and we move at a slower pace. Less rushed and more of a prolonged burn. I realize it as he's kissing his way over my neck, down my collarbone, and groping my breasts with a reverence he doesn't hide. He's making love to me.

"Lawson," I groan his name, and he rumbles an appreciative sound in response.

My fingers tangle in his hair, tugging as he sends me off into oblivion, shattering around him with the most intense orgasm of my life. When I come back down, he grabs my face, staring into my eyes until his release severs the connection. I swallow the sound of pleasure from his lips and squeeze around him, collapsing into his chest.

His fingers move to that blank space on the back of my neck, stroking me, and I know what he's thinking before he even says it.

"This was always meant to be mine."

"Then brand me already," I challenge him. "Take it because it's yours."

He tips my chin up, pulling back to meet my gaze. "Tonight."

"What?" I blink at him, not certain I heard him correctly.

"Tonight," he repeats. "I don't want to wait

another day. Marry me, Mercedes. Let me claim you the way I should have a long fucking time ago."

The intensity in his eyes unravels me, and as crazy as it sounds, I find myself nodding along because it's the only thing that makes sense.

"Tonight," I murmur my agreement, my fingers moving reverently over his face. "Make me yours, Lawson Montgomery. And don't ever let me go again."

20

MERCEDES

The benefit of Judge being a Sovereign Son is that his word can move mountains. In the span of time it takes for me to shower and do my hair and makeup, he's already got an army assembled downstairs in my condo.

There's a moment of surprise when I see Solana, Georgie, Ivy, and Santiago are all waiting for me. But that moment is quickly swept up in the chaos as Solana and Ivy usher me upstairs to try on wedding dresses.

"Don't worry." Solana starts fingering through the hanging bags on the rack they set up in the nursery. "I gave the stylist a brief rundown of your style."

I can see that, and I'm glad for it. Because only a few dresses in the whole display are white. The others are golds, blacks, emerald greens, and most importantly, red. Specifically, crimson. That's the first one I see. The first one that beckons me, and when I pull it out to examine it, I already know this will be the one.

"Solana." My gratitude falls from my lips on a quiet breath.

"I know." She smiles. "But I can't take all the credit. I have to say, if having designer dresses delivered on demand is one of the perks of The Society, I'm totally on board for that benefit."

Ivy and I both laugh, and Solana helps me remove the gown from the bag before holding it up to me. The garment is stunning, a rich velvet piece with off-the-shoulder straps. It's simple but elegant and will show off my pregnancy, so I suspect Judge will love it. But first, I have to get into the thing.

When I start to remove my robe, Solana heads back to the rack, rifling through some pieces on the end section before she tosses me a lacy black pair of underwear and a strapless bra.

"For the wedding night," she says slyly. "Although I have a feeling you two have already celebrated, judging by the flush on your cheeks."

The flush spreads as I give her my back and slip the bra and panties on.

"We're going to have to catch up on all this, by the way," Ivy says. "But there isn't time tonight because apparently your lawman is in a big hurry to drag you down the aisle."

I close my eyes, the warmth of that reality

moving through me all over again. A part of me still wonders if it's a dream. If this is crazy. But the other part of me, the one that loves him with my whole heart, doesn't care. I want him. He finally admitted he wants me too, so there is no point for us to wait. I want to do this. I want to be Lawson Montgomery's wife. So I get it. I understand this mad rush. Honestly, I wouldn't even care if we were married in our street clothes. But Judge told me he wants to do it right, and that means something.

So here I am, pouring myself into a dress that somehow fits just right. It's a dress that immediately brings tears to Solana's and Ivy's eyes, and when they lead me to the mirror, it brings tears to mine too.

"Okay stop it." Solana waves her hands in front of her face. "I really don't want to redo my makeup."

"I'm sorry," I blubber. "I can't help it."

We're all half laughing, half crying when Georgie appears carrying a selection of bouquets for me to choose from. I recognize them all as flowers from his shop, and I've never been so grateful to have friends who understand my tastes so well.

"They're stunning." I finger the flowers, settling on a bouquet of champagne roses.

"As are you." Georgie leans in to kiss my cheek, and my emotions come back in a big way.

"Okay, you guys seriously have to stop," Solana yelps. "Shoes... we need shoes!"

"Stilettos," I tell her, trying to focus on the task at hand.

"Really?" Georgie asks. "You've been whining about your feet being swollen for days."

"It'll just be for the wedding." I shrug.

He rolls his eyes. "The things women put themselves through."

Lucky for me, Solana understands, and she helps me pick out the perfect pair of black stilettos, albeit a size larger than I'd typically wear. After that, there isn't much left to do, but Santiago appears at the door, and everyone seems to sense he wants a moment of privacy with me. So they all take their leave without being asked, shutting the door behind them.

His eyes move over me, uncharacteristically charged with emotion, and he swallows audibly before speaking. "You look beautiful, Mercedes."

"Thank you," I choke out. "Will you walk me down the aisle?"

His features soften, something passing through his eyes, and he nods. "This is what you want then?"

"It is." There can be no doubt to my words, and I know Santi sees that.

"I'm proud of you," he says quietly. "I want you to know that. You're going to be an amazing mother and wife. And Judge will be a good husband to you. If he isn't, he knows I'll kill him myself."

He says it in a way that someone might take as a

joke, except I know Santiago is dead serious. It only makes me love him more.

"Thank you, brother." I hug him, lowering my voice to a whisper. "I love you."

"I love you too." He pulls back after a moment, seemingly trying to steel himself before he hands me a familiar velvet box. "Judge asked me to give this to you."

I open it with a smile and slip the necklace on, my fingers grazing the chain as it settles against my skin.

A gentle knock on the door interrupts the moment, and Ivy pokes her head in with an apologetic smile. "The cars are here. Judge said he wants you with him, so you'll have to wear this until we get to the church."

I recognize the cloak as one he wears at IVI, and it brings me comfort as I slip it over my shoulders, his scent surrounding me. Usually, these are reserved for men, but there's no way Judge is letting me out of his sight right now. So this will conceal my dress until the actual ceremony.

Once I have it in place, Santiago takes me by the arm and leads me downstairs to join my groom. He looks more handsome than a man has a right to standing there in his black tux and matching crimson tie and pocket square. Something I'm assuming is also Solana's doing.

At the bottom of the stairs, Santi reluctantly

hands me over to Judge, and we all make our way out to the convoy of vehicles that will deliver us to the IVI compound. Judge helps me into our private car, his hand squeezing mine as we begin the journey. The privacy screen is up, and I'm grateful for it when Judge turns to me.

"You look beautiful," he murmurs, his lips pressing against my temple.

"You haven't even seen my dress yet." I smile in amusement.

"It doesn't matter," he answers seriously. "You always look beautiful. But never more so than you do with our babies inside you. When my ring is on your finger, and my mark is inked into your skin, I'll never want to take my eyes off you."

The possession that burns in his voice heats me from within, and I know the journey is short, but I can't help myself. I unbuckle and crawl onto his lap, reaching for his zipper. His eyes flare with want, and he grunts his approval as I free his cock and lift the fabric of the dress and cloak around me. Within seconds, I've got him inside me again, and we're going at it hot and heavy all the way to the church. We both come hard, Judge continuing to grind my body down onto his long after the last convulsion has rocked through him. And when his eyes meet mine, I know this is just the beginning. He isn't even close to being done with me tonight.

"Now you'll have my come dripping down your

thighs as you join me at the altar." He brushes his lips against my ear, kissing his way down my jaw, and I shiver.

"Mm-hmm."

His hands continue to stroke my ass, even after the car comes to a stop, and we hear the commotion of everyone gathering outside. Someone knocks on the window, but we ignore them, Judge bringing my lips to his, kissing me like we have all the time in the world. I think we do too, until I hear another persistent knock, followed by Solana's chagrined voice.

"You better not be messing up her hair, Lawson Montgomery!"

He chuckles, shaking his head, and I smile. After we right our clothing and he helps me out, Solana ensnares me with a disapproving look.

"Nice." She rolls her eyes. "I didn't realize freshly fucked chic was the look we were going for."

I shrug. "As if you wouldn't have done the same."

"Who knows, maybe I will." Her eyes scan the crowd before turning back to Judge. "Is your asshole brother here tonight?"

At her question, I stiffen, and Judge settles his hand on my lower back. He doesn't answer her, but nods to the crowd filtering inside. "We better go in."

I'm grateful for the interruption in that conversation, but I make a mental note to talk to Solana about Theron later. Again.

Judge guides me inside while Solana wanders

back to the others, presumably to boss people around and make sure everything's in order. And then all too soon, we are separated with little more than time for a kiss, taken to our own separate areas to get ready. Although there isn't much for me to do than remove the cloak and visit with Ivy, Georgie, and Solana, who's fussing over my hair that she insists I messed up during our pre-wedding romp.

I'm on a cloud, too happy to care about anything. I remain that way when Santi comes to get me, leading me to the large doors as we wait for the music to begin. A moment later, they open, and things happen, most of which I'm not fully aware of. For all I know, they could be playing heavy metal. Because all I see is the man waiting for me at the altar. My handsome, crazy, intense husband-to-be.

The journey to him feels too long, but somehow, I get there. Santi releases me, taking his place at Judge's side, while Solana stands at mine. The priest opens with a prayer, and I stare into Judge's eyes, bathing in the warm glow. Admittedly, a part of me worried he might still be nervous or uncertain. But right now, all I can see is determination and pride.

The ceremony is a traditionally Catholic one, like all Society weddings, although a condensed version, given that it's already almost midnight. Even so, a whole host of our acquaintances, friends, and family are gathered for the occasion, along with the witnesses from IVI bearing their masks and cloaks.

If I'm being honest, I don't hear half of what the priest says. Not until it's time to say our vows and exchange rings. My ring is a stunning pavé diamond band with an eye-catching centerpiece to match the design of the necklace Judge gave me. It's perfect in every way, and I feel proud to have his ring on my finger, but I'm even happier to see the white gold band on his.

With that rite complete, finally, after what feels like an eternity, the priest declares us husband and wife. Judge doesn't wait for approval to sweep me into his arms and kiss me with a deep growl that I'm quite certain the entire church heard. But I don't mind one bit, and I kiss him right back, far longer than what's considered appropriate. It isn't until my brother clears his throat that Judge seems to remember we have an audience.

"Save it for later, will you?" Santi mutters.

Judge releases my lips from his, but his warmth doesn't fade as his eyes roam over me.

"I love you," he says again, low enough for me to hear, a stolen moment of privacy while we're surrounded by others.

"I love you too." I smile up at him, my heart beating a crazy new song just for him. "So very much, Lawson Montgomery."

The priest interrupts our exchange with instructions to greet those who have gathered here this evening. We do so together, hand in hand, Judge never releasing me as we accept congratulations from far too many people.

I don't miss their curious glances, particularly at my very obvious pregnancy. I'm sure this news will have tongues wagging later, but they don't dare say a word to Judge about it now. Of course, when we greet Giordana, Dulce, and Vivien, they don't bother to hide their disdain. It doesn't escape my notice that Vivien is wearing black as if she's in mourning, her eyes moving over me sharply.

When she leans in for an air kiss and a frigid hug, her biting words penetrate my ear. "Well, I guess that's one way to secure a husband."

By the tightening of Judge's hand on mine, it's clear he's heard the remark too, and he doesn't miss a beat.

"You are mistaken, Vivien." His eyes move over me with undiluted admiration. "It was me who needed to secure Mercedes's hand. There's no other woman who can compare."

Vivien looks as if she's been slapped by Judge's remark, and it pleases me far more than it should when we leave her standing there, mouth agape as we walk away.

"I think I've had enough congratulations for the moment," Judge says.

I nod in agreement as he leads me toward the door, pausing for a moment to look at me.

"Are you sure you want to do this tonight?"

He's referring to the mark. The tattoo he will ink into my skin himself. We discussed it briefly, along with a phone call to an IVI doctor. It's not exactly common to give the mark to pregnant wives, but it has been done before, and with the proper precautions and sterile equipment, we have the green light to proceed if we wish.

"I want it now," I assure him. "More than anything."

His eyes flare with that possession again, and he nods. "Okay, little monster. As you wish."

He directs me to the church doors that lead into the IVI courtyard. I already know from experience that another gathering will witness him giving me the mark. Yet it will be an intimate moment. His hands on my body. His artistry on my skin. His claim on me for all of eternity.

A frisson of excitement moves through me as an attendant opens the doors for us to step outside. My head is in the clouds, the starry sky above twinkling just for us. There isn't a single moment of tonight I would change. It feels magical. It feels like I'm on a roller coaster going a million miles an hour, the wind in my hair, the thrill of the destination ahead on my mind. Everything is perfect. It's beautiful. It's amazing.

Until it isn't.

Judge freezes beside me, and I look up at him, following his gaze to a man at the bottom of the stairs. He's not familiar to me, but I don't have to guess who he is as he raises his arm, the glint of silver in the moonlight aimed straight at me.

It all seems to happen in slow motion. The choked word from Judge as he shoves me behind him. The pop that splits the air, piercing the perfect bubble we had only a moment ago. Warm liquid splatters my face, and I feel myself falling, Judge's body jerking against mine. In the chaos, I catch a glimpse of Vincent's shoes as they move toward us, echoing like the executioner he is. I cling to Judge, silent tears streaming down my face as I realize we're never going to meet our babies. This is it. The beginning and the end.

"No!" Someone screams, and there's a flash of a familiar robe. A masked man from the wedding tackles Vincent to the ground, and then there are two more quick pops, followed by a grunt, and one final gunshot ringing through the night air.

I see Vincent's head loll to the side, half of his face blown open. Screams tear through the crowd, followed by more chaos as people move around us. But it all fades away when I turn to Judge, reaching for his face. I want to tell him it's going to be okay. Except it's wrong. It's all wrong.

His eyes are closed, his breathing shallow, and when I roll him onto his back, I understand why. Blood seeps from his head, dripping down his neck.

"Judge?" I shake him in a panic, but he doesn't respond.

"Judge!" I scream, the strange voice coming from my lips unfamiliar. "No! You can't do this to me! I just got you back!"

Sobs rack my body as a pair of strong arms come around me, trying to pry me away.

"Mercedes." Santi's pained voice infiltrates my anguish. "Come. We have to get you out of here."

"No!" I scream at the top of my lungs, throwing myself over Judge, but Santi pulls me back again, kicking and screaming.

"We just got married," I sob. "He can't leave me now. We're supposed to have forever, Santi. Tell me we're going to have forever."

"I'm sorry," Santi chokes out. "Mercedes, I'm so fucking sorry."

21

JUDGE

I see him the instant we step outside. Through the happy chaos of our wedding as bells ring in this late hour and the inky blue sky sparkles, he is here, lost among the witnesses collected in the courtyard for this next part of the ceremony. The placing of my mark on the back of my wife's neck in that space I've known, on some level, was for me. Was always for me.

Mercedes feels the shift in me. I sense it in how her back stiffens. Don't the others see him? But the scene is confusing; too many people here to watch the wedding that I swore would never be, the gates less well-guarded in the rushed mess of it. And Vincent Douglas standing in a borrowed or more likely stolen, ill-fitting cloak, his shoes too loud, his hatred too palpable.

In the throng, he stands apart. It's as if the others

sense his menace and keep their distance. But they don't see his eyes. No one does. They're all watching my beautiful wife in all her happiness.

In a happiness we were perhaps never meant to have.

Mercedes senses the shift in my body and looks up at me. My hands move over the swell of her stomach, and I see her confused face in my periphery. Because my eyes are locked on him. The gunman who pushes the robe back, the weapon catching the light, polished metal glinting as shiny as it is deadly.

All the noise and laughter become background. A throbbing, muted thing as Vincent Douglas raises his arm, the robe falling away fully. A choked *no* escapes me as I push Mercedes behind me, and I swear I see the burst of light as the gun fires.

A scream. Someone finally screams.

No, that's not right. The scream comes after. After the white-hot pain. After I'm falling. Mercedes.

A man calls out. There are two more pops, then a third. More shrieks, people confused and afraid.

"Judge!" It's Mercedes. Her voice sounds strange, not like herself. She's shaking me. "Judge! No! You can't do this to me! I just got you back."

I want to reach out for her, but I can't seem to move. Can't open my eyes. I want to tell her it will be okay, but I don't think it will. I think it's too late for that. Too late to have a marriage with the woman I love. Too late for our little family. For me to be the man I was meant to be all along.

It's when she's dragged off me that I feel the cold loss of her, and finally, finally, the throbbing pain subsides, and I am gone.

22

SANTIAGO

Mercedes kicks and screams, thrusting her elbows into my gut as I hand her off to Marco. "Take them home! Lock her in her room if you have to!"

Ivy is already in the car and he's hauling Mercedes into it. He pushes in beside her and the driver takes off before he's even closed the door. I see her nearly crawl over his lap to get out. To get to her husband. And the misery on her face breaks my heart.

She just got this. They just got here. After everything, they finally arrived at the start of their happily ever after. But I don't know if a De La Rosa or a Montgomery is destined to have a happy ending. I hope I'm wrong for my sister's sake. For my daughter's sake. But I don't trust fate. And as I drop to my knees beside my friend, I send a curse up to the heavens for what they've allowed to happen on this night of all nights.

"Call a motherfucking ambulance!"

"It's on its way," a man says as I rip away Judge's tie, his shirt. He's going to fucking choke. There's so much blood I can't fucking tell where it's coming from. "Mr. De La Rosa, stop," the same man says as I give Judge a shake. "You'll do more harm than good. Move back."

I realize it's Dr. Barnes, and he's pressing a bloodred cloth to the wound on Judge's head.

Blood red. It's the handkerchief from Judge's pocket. It was to match my sister's wedding dress. But the red was never meant to be fucking blood.

"Judge, you wake the hell up, you hear me!"

"Someone get him away from here!" Barnes orders angrily, and two sets of arms haul me up as the sirens that were too distant just minutes ago are close enough to drown out the screams of the women.

For a moment, I'm transported back in time to the night of the masquerade ball. The night similar sounds broke into that of elegant music and crystal flutes overflowing with champagne clinking together in celebration. The night I almost died.

"He's not breathing," a paramedic calls out as I'm hauled away from my friend, but I realize he's not the only one hurt. The other man, the one who shot

Vincent Douglas dead, he's the one who's not breathing.

"Jesus Christ. Get the fuck off me!" I rip away from the men holding me and take in the gruesome sight at the bottom of the stairs. Vincent Douglas lies dead, half his face blown off. And beside him, the masked, cloaked man who shot him. Who probably saved my sister's life. Judge's too. If he survives.

I bend to push off his mask as the paramedics work, yelling for me to back away. I recognize him although it's been years. At least five. More?

"Theron?"

"Sir, move away."

I look behind me to find a stretcher being rolled over and watch as they lift Theron's limp body onto it on the count of three. They push past me, two stretchers going toward the waiting ambulance, both brothers quiet, unmoving.

I go after them, grab a paramedic by the arm and make him face me. "Are they going to make it?"

The other man slams the door.

"Sir, we need to go. Now!"

"I'm riding with you."

"There's no room!" The other door is slammed shut, and the driver takes off.

"Fuck!" I push my hands into my hair and look around at the chaos of my sister's wedding. A night that's turned the courtyard of IVI bloodier than it's ever been. Bloodier than perhaps that scaffold that stands concealed but ready in the small, grassy area behind The Tribunal building.

I need a car. I need a fucking car.

"Sir! Santiago!" I spin to find Raul, Judge's driver, rushing toward me. "I'll take you to the hospital. This way."

I follow him to his Rolls—the one Judge and Mercedes rode in—and we drive at breakneck speed toward the hospital, the sirens that were fading growing louder when we pull into the lot just as they're unloading the Montgomery brothers.

Fuck. Both of them like this. Both unconscious. Surely, the gods cannot be this cruel, but they are. I know that well.

"Thank you," I tell Raul.

"Sir, his wife?" he asks. "He'll want her here."

I stop, think, then nod. "Yes. Okay. I'll make a call. She's at De La Rosa Manor."

"I'll bring her."

I text Marco as I rush into the hospital to let him know Raul is coming for Mercedes. I can just imagine how crazed she must be right now. How panicked. She was prepared to raise her children on her own. It took so long for Judge to get to this point. To marry her. And it feels like fate has betrayed her doubly. To hang that future in front of her eyes only to snatch it away so violently.

No. I cannot think like this.

He will survive. He will make it. He has to. His

brother, though, he looked really bad, the skin of his face an unnatural gray.

"Where are the Montgomery brothers? They were in the ambulance that just came in," I say to the woman at the reception desk. She should know them. This is a Society hospital.

She takes a look at me, and I glance down, seeing the smear of Judge's blood on me. Given that and the half-skull tattoo on my face, I understand the panic on hers. But I don't care. I slam my hands on the counter.

"Where the fuck are they?"

"Surgery. Surgery rooms six and seven."

"Mr. De La Rosa." I turn to find Dr. Barnes hurrying in through the sliding glass doors. He gives the woman at the desk a nod and takes my arm. "Come with me. I'll take you where we can wait."

"My sister. She's on her way."

He turns to the woman at the desk. "Make sure Mrs. Montgomery is taken to waiting room one."

Mrs. Montgomery. She has barely been that for a few minutes. Will she be a widow already?

Jesus Christ.

"Sir, let's go. I can check in and let you know what's going on in surgery."

I nod and let him lead me to a waiting room that is meant to be comfortable and welcoming. I doubt it provides either comfort or welcome to those who must wait here, though. And tonight, it's all pacing and watching that damn screen with information that never seems to fucking update. I remember the last time I sat in this waiting room and watched the same board for news on Ivy. When I was sure I'd lost her.

Fate has been ugly to us.

"Santi?" Mercedes's choked voice breaks into my dark reverie. I turn to see her still in her dress, blood still smeared on her face, dark across the chest of the crimson dress, the swell of her stomach. Her makeup is smeared, and she's crying.

I go to her, take her in my arms and hold her tight as her body is wracked by sobs too violent for any human being to bear.

23

JUDGE

I wake with a headache that rivals any I've ever had.

A gasp nearby has me turn my head in that direction but opening my eyes seems to present a challenge I am not up for.

"Judge!" It's Mercedes. Her voice breaks on my name as both of her hands close around one of mine. I drag my eyes open, the light so bright behind her it's painful, but in that light, she looks so lovely, so like an angel with a sweep of dark hair cascading around her. I smell her shampoo when she leans closer to peer at me. For a moment, I wonder if I haven't died. If we haven't died. "Judge," she says again more quietly this time as she sucks in three short breaths. Tears mar her beautiful angel's face. She looks like she's been crying for days.

"We must be dead," I manage as I reach up to

brush my fingers over her face and wipe away some of those tears. I have seen too many of them during these past months.

She laughs and shakes her head. Her hair caresses my cheek, and it's the best feeling ever.

"We're not dead, but you tried. Why would you do that? Put yourself in front of a bullet like that?" Here come those tears again as she sits down and lays her head on my chest, hands squeezing one of mine.

"What would you have had me do? Let you take it? Let our children—" I don't finish that thought.

"Oh, Judge. I thought you were dead. I thought… all the blood. There was so much blood." She raises her head and brings her face close. A tear falls on my cheek, and she kisses it away.

I know I can move my arms, so I wiggle my toes and take stock of my body. Apart from my head feeling like it weighs about a thousand pounds and a tight sensation along the side of it, I think I'm alright.

"What happened after I went down? Is everyone okay?"

She kisses my mouth and brushes my hair away from my forehead. She doesn't quite answer me, though, and I see how her eyes travel over my face, not holding mine.

"Mercedes?" I want to sit up, alert suddenly. I try but fuck my head.

"Just lie down, Judge. You took a bullet, for God's sake. Just lie down."

"Tell me."

The door opens, and she turns. I look too and find Santiago entering. He sees that I'm awake and smiles, but there's a darkness to the set of his features, too.

"Mercedes? You're alright?" I ask her. "Did he hurt you?" She shakes her head, more tears. "The babies. Is it the babies?"

"No, they're fine, Judge. We're fine. And you're going to be fine. The bullet grazed your skull, but there was just a lot of blood, and it looked much worse than it was."

Santiago puts his hand on his sister's back, and he looks freshly showered. He must have gone home after they brought me here. I wonder how much time has passed.

"Is someone going to tell me what the fuck is going on?" I ask them.

Mercedes looks up at Santiago, and I know it's bad. But how bad can it be? It's not Ivy, or he wouldn't be here. Elena wasn't at the wedding. I take inventory of the rest of the guests. Who would have Mercedes looking like she's looking?

"Is it Solana or Georgie? Did something happen to them?" I realize how I've come to care about them weirdly. Especially Solana.

"No, Judge they're fine. And you'll be fine. You

have a concussion and about a dozen stitches. They did shave the side of your head, which is not a look I recommend keeping," Santiago says, trying to make things light, but I know the worst is coming. "You were lucky. A centimeter to the right and..."

He doesn't have to finish. I'd be dead. Mercedes made a widow on the day she's a bride.

"Vincent Douglas is dead," Mercedes says. She looks stricken at this.

"Who killed him?"

They exchange a dark look between them. This is what they don't want to tell me.

"Who?" I ask, pushing through the pain to prop myself up on my elbows.

They both look at me for a long moment, and Mercedes finally answers. And I understand why she's crying.

"Theron."

Theron?

No.

My brother wasn't invited to the wedding. He wasn't to show his face at the compound. My brother whom I've been keeping at arm's length. Whom I haven't yet forgiven for what he did to Mercedes. Who has been trying to rebuild bridges.

"He's in critical condition. He came out of surgery just a couple of hours ago."

"Couple of hours?"

"He took two bullets at close range before he

managed to kill Douglas. The damage was... extensive. Surgery lasted about eleven hours."

"Jesus Christ. Where is he? I want to see him." I try to push off the bed, but the room spins, and two sets of hands push me back down.

"You need to rest, Judge. Your head—"

"A couple of stitches and a concussion I'll survive. I want to see my brother. Take me to my brother."

Santiago nods and leaves the room. Mercedes holds on to me, crying silent tears. And I know from that it's not looking good for him.

Santiago reenters the room pushing a wheelchair, a nurse on his heels. "Sir, he isn't ready to be moved."

"Tell him that," Santiago says.

Mercedes gets up, moves her chair out of the way and pushes the blanket off my thighs. I'm grateful to be wearing a hospital gown and a pair of pajama bottoms.

"Lois brought those for you," she says. I would have put the top on too but—"

"It's fine." I squeeze her hand. "Thank you."

Santiago looks at me disapprovingly but helps me sit up, which is an effort, then helps me into the chair, which he pushes as the nurse clicks her tongue, threatening to tell the doctor. Does she think any of us give a fuck?

Mercedes walks beside me, and I hold her hand,

turning her wedding ring around and around, trying to understand what we did to deserve this as our punishment. This horror on our wedding day.

But I can live with that. I think she can too.

At the end of the hall, we turn into the private room where machines beep all around my brother, breathing for him, pumping his heart, monitoring every minuscule shift in him as he lies helpless on the bed, eyes closed, a tube taped to his mouth to give him breath.

I can live with the horror of that wedding day.

But what I can't live with is my brother dying before I can tell him I forgive him and that I'm sorry I haven't been the brother he needed for so long.

24

JUDGE

I am released later that night but only leave well after midnight, when I'm dead on my feet and can't keep my eyes open. Still, Mercedes has to drag me out of my brother's room.

When we get home, we find Lois waiting in the kitchen, and she hugs us both. It's a little awkward for me, but Mercedes seems to give herself over to it. I realize how she has come to trust Lois. How their bond has grown.

She makes us eat a plate of food before she'll let us go up to bed, which is probably a good thing, especially for Mercedes.

"How are you, really?" I ask Mercedes when we're alone.

She reaches out to touch the side of my head where the hair is shaved, brushing a gentle finger across the stitches.

"I'm okay. We're okay," she says. She drinks the cup of orange juice, and a few moments later, she smiles a sad smile. She takes my hand and sets it on her stomach.

"Sugar rush," I say as I feel the kicking of two sets of feet or hands. I don't know which. "Does it hurt you?"

"No. I love it, actually."

"It was supposed to be a beautiful night for you."

"It's okay, Judge. I don't care about that."

"I know you don't, but for so long, you've had so much sadness, and I wanted it for you."

She shrugs a shoulder. "I'll survive." She looks down. I know why. She's thinking about Theron. Because he may not survive. The best doctors worked on him, but, as Santiago said, two close-range shots did a lot of damage. Too much, maybe.

"He's strong." I touch her cheek with one finger and lift her face up to mine. "And stubborn as hell."

She laughs at that. "Why do you think he did it? I mean, he must have known he could get hurt... or worse."

I consider this. I have been thinking about it for hours. Why did he do it? Sacrifice himself for a brother to whom he came asking forgiveness and received none. A brother he tried to mend his relationship with, but I wouldn't give him the chance. A brother who did not even invite him to his wedding.

"He's been wanting to apologize to you. He came to see me, but I wouldn't let him go near you."

She nods. "He's made an impression on Solana."

"Well, when he wakes, we'll tell him that because, weirdly, after she stomped on his foot and probably caused some damage with that heel of hers, he hasn't stopped asking about her."

We both chuckle.

"Masochist," she says.

"Let's go up to our room." I stand.

That makes her pause, then nod. She slips off her stool and slides her arm into mine. We walk side by side up the stairs and to my bedroom. When we turn on the lights, we are both surprised to see it's been decorated with hundreds of roses and candles, although they're unlit, and crimson petals on the bed.

"This must be Georgie. Probably with Lois's help," Mercedes says.

"Let's just go to sleep. I'll ask Lois to remove everything tomorrow."

"No, don't. We'll take them to Theron. It'll be nice for him to wake up to a cheery room."

"That's a good idea." Neither of us mentions that he may not wake up at all.

We undress each other, and I brush the petals off the bed before we slide in side by side, husband and wife, and sleep. Mercedes curls into me, pressing her belly against my side. It's not how I expected to spend my first night with my wife in my bed, but this is our reality.

We're alive. Unhurt, mostly. Theron wasn't so lucky. So I close my eyes with a thank you on my lips as I tug her close and ask the gods who have been so cruel until now to grant me one wish. To let my brother wake up and walk out of that hospital himself. And when he does, I promise to take him back. To forgive and finally forget all that's come to pass. To thank him. To try to understand him.

25

MERCEDES

"Are you sure you want to do this?" Judge cups my face, his eyes searching mine.

"Yes." I wrap my arms around his waist and give him a light squeeze.

He still doesn't look convinced, but enough time has passed, and I've grown tired of being separated from him far too often these last few weeks. Our marriage didn't come with the honeymoon we'd hoped for, and when Judge hasn't been at the hospital with Theron, he's catching up on work.

It's clear he still carries guilt over what happened. The lingering tensions between the two brothers before Theron almost died certainly doesn't help. And while I thought I'd be the last person ever feeling indebted to Theron in any way, I can't deny the truth. He hurt me. He terrified me. But he also gave me the greatest gift anyone ever has. In a split-second decision, he undoubtedly saved Judge's life, as well as that of our babies. If it wasn't for Theron, I could have been spending my honeymoon at my husband's grave, mourning his loss rather than planning our future together.

It's an admission that rocks me to my core. And admittedly, I still feel a rush of fear every time he leaves the house. Or if he doesn't come home exactly on time. If he takes too long to text me back. I know these things will get better in time, but right now, I can't help it. I want to be near him. I need to be near him. I can't be at ease unless I feel his presence beside me.

"You look tired," Judge observes, his thumbs brushing over my cheeks. "Perhaps you should stay home and rest."

"Says the man who hardly sleeps." I reach up and stroke my fingers through the back of his hair. "I'm tired because I'm growing two tiny humans inside me. But I'm also tired of resting. I want to go with you."

He still seems reluctant, and I know why. While I'm desperate to have him near me as much as possible, he's desperate to keep me at home where he knows I'm safe. It hasn't escaped me that every time he looks at me, he carries the burden of additional guilt for that too. In some way, he still feels like he failed to protect me even though he'd done all he could. I've told him again and again that what happened couldn't be avoided. Vincent was determined, and even if someone had thwarted his attempt that night, he would have found another time and place. I understand that, but I think it will take Judge time to come to terms with it.

"This isn't how I'd imagined us spending this time," he says. "But I want you to know that when this is over, you'll get your honeymoon. You'll get everything you want."

"All I want is you." I offer him a warm smile. "I'm easy to please."

He smirks as if it's the furthest thing from the truth he's ever heard, and I slap his chest.

"Hey, I am."

"Don't worry." He leans in, his lips hovering over mine. "I like you demanding. Particularly when you're in our bed."

I melt into him, wishing we had more time to go do exactly that. My hormones have been insane, and even though I'm uncomfortable ninety percent of the time, I can't seem to get enough of Judge. I know I've been exhausting him more when he comes home at night and I reach for him in the dark, scrambling to get him any way I can. But he hasn't complained, so I figure it's fair play.

"Later," he promises in a raspy voice, clearly amused by the longing in my expression.

And with that dark assurance, he takes me by the hand and leads me to the car. Raul drives us to The

Society hospital that's housed Theron during his recovery, but I know Judge has been making alternate plans. Theron will need rehabilitation, and Judge has sought out the best team for that part of his recovery as well. I don't know when they'll be moving him, but I suspect it will be soon.

When we arrive, a strange flutter of nerves erupts in my belly as Judge leads me to Theron's room. Quite honestly, I never thought I'd have to face him again. I never wanted to. But I know now, after Judge confirmed Theron has been struggling with addiction, that he's been battling his own demons. It isn't an excuse for what happened, but at least in a way, I can understand.

I am not without sin myself, and if I were following my religious scruples, I shouldn't be the one to cast stones. In other words, I've done some pretty fucked-up things in my own life, and coming from that place, I understand there has to be space for forgiveness. Not only for his sake, but my own.

"You can always change your mind." Judge stops at the door with Theron's name beside it, his hand squeezing mine. "I'll take you home right now if you want."

"No." I force a smile and shake my head. "I want to do this."

He nods, but the concern doesn't leave his eyes. And then, just like we're ripping off a Band-Aid, he opens the door, and we step inside.

I don't know what I'm expecting exactly, considering the severity of Theron's injuries and the fact that he barely scraped through. In my head, I imagined him lying prone in his bed, barely able to fend for himself. Yet the scene before us is anything but a helpless man.

He is in his bed, of course, but he's propped up by a stack of pillows behind him. The low murmur of the television plays in the background, but he's not focused on that. No, his attention is on the two pretty nurses at his side, one fussing over his food while the other shaves his face. Both of them wearing smiles entirely too large.

Judge arches a brow at the scene just as Theron returns it with a devilish grin. That grin falters briefly as he turns his attention to me, and something shifts in the room. I feel it in the shiver that moves over my spine, the memory of that awful night not too distant.

In some ways, it feels like a lifetime ago. But in others, the wound feels fresh because it hasn't been dealt with. Not really. When I came to face him, I knew it wasn't going to be easy. But this charming version of Theron is the one that I first met. The man with the handsome features and easy smile. A quick wit, which he's obviously been using to entertain the nurses. All of these details were so non-threatening that I quickly warmed to him. But I know, even now with his eyes clear and the solemn expression that falls over him, he still has demons to battle.

"Thank you, ladies," Theron says dismissively. "Let's resume this another time."

The nurses glance at us, trying and failing to adopt a professional demeanor before they quickly shuffle out of the room at his command. I have an urge to roll my eyes, but I don't. Because Theron's are still locked on me, and I know he has something to say before he even begins.

"Mercedes." He nods at me. "I'm flattered you'd come to see me. Unless... perhaps, you were hoping I was really dead?"

Though his voice has a teasing lilt, there is a hint of vulnerability beneath it. Like maybe that's what he expects from everyone in his life. That we'd all wish that for him.

"Actually, no. That's not why I'm here."

Judge tucks me against his side protectively, his hand wrapping around my lower back to settle on the curve of my hip. An awkward silence falls over the room, and then Theron sits up straighter, wincing as he does.

"I owe you an apology," he confesses. "And if you'll hear me out, I'd like to give that to you now."

"It's not necessary." I lean into Judge, grateful for the strength of his body right now. "I don't want your apology."

Disappointment flashes through Theron's eyes as

they drift to my very pregnant belly, and I can only wonder if he's thinking about what he'll miss out on. That he'll always be distant from his family.

"Mercedes—" he tries again, but I shake my head and cut him off.

"I don't want your apology because we're even," I tell him. "You saved our lives. You saved Judge's life. And for that..." I stumble over the words, almost too choked up to speak. "I'm grateful."

He shifts, clearly uncomfortable by the display of emotion, and at that moment, I see so many similarities between him and Judge. And I can't help feeling a pang of warmth toward him. Naturally, Theron being a Montgomery, he has to ruin that.

"I suppose I am due some credit," he says thoughtfully. "You can repay me by naming one of your spawns after me."

Judge snorts, and I shake my head. And just like that, some of the tension dissolves.

"Not in this lifetime, brother." Judge takes a seat in one of the visitor's chairs, pulling me down onto his lap.

"Fine." Theron grins wickedly, turning his gaze to me. "Then I have a counter suggestion. I'm in need of a good nurse. Perhaps you know someone?"

"It seems to me you have two very doting nurses on hand already," I answer wryly.

He shrugs dismissively. "They'll do in a pinch,

but I'd prefer someone with a little more bark. Perhaps even some bite."

I don't have to guess where this is going, and he confirms it with his next words.

"A fiery shop owner. What's her name again?"

"As if you don't know," Judge mutters. "You couldn't handle her. Trust me."

Theron's eyes alight with pleasure at the insinuation. "Now you're goading me. You know I love a challenge."

"She's off-limits," I tell him. "Seriously. That's a no-go zone."

Judge groans, looking at me like I just made a crucial mistake. "Now he'll never let it go."

"You know me well," Theron muses.

"Why don't you just focus on your recovery?" Judge suggests. "Then you can concentrate on your baser needs."

Theron smirks, wisely choosing to change the subject, probably sensing I might strangle him if he goes near Solana. Regardless, we fall into an easy discussion about the impending babies, and he seems to hold a genuine interest in the subject, which surprises me. He's curious about our name choices and even makes a bet with himself on the genders, which will be revealed next week at my baby shower. Oddly enough, it seems like he's looking forward to being an uncle. And although I'm nowhere close to being able to trust him, I feel like we're rebuilding a bridge between him and Judge. Theron wants to be a part of his life and, by extension, his children's. And I think as long as things continue to go smoothly, we can make that happen.

By the time we leave several hours later, Judge and I are both exhausted. Yet his rough promise lingers in the back of my mind when he gets me upstairs to our bedroom back at home.

I unbutton his shirt, sliding my hands over his warm chest while he watches me reverently, the same way he does every time I do this. It's become a habit, like opening a gift every day, and I have no plans to stop anytime soon. Secretly, I think he likes it when I have my way with him just as much as I like it when he does the same to me.

Slowly, I unzip his trousers, easing my hand in to stroke his cock. He bites back a groan, his eyes shuttering as he whispers a low warning.

"Mercedes."

I ignore him, sitting on the bed as I continue stroking him. He's been trying to be gentle with me the further along I get. His words, not mine. Yet I'm always testing him. I don't want him to be gentle even though I understand his reasons for it. I just want my Judge. Rough and growly and possessive in all the ways that count.

My tongue darts out to swirl around the head of his cock, and his chest rumbles in approval. Despite his best efforts, his hand tangles in my hair as I draw him into my mouth, sucking him with a torturous slowness.

Another sound gets caught in his throat as his grip on me tightens, and he inevitably gets caught up in it the way I knew he would. He shoves my face deeper, his cock lodging in the back of my throat, making my eyes water as he glares down at me.

"Is this what you wanted?" he growls.

I smile and try to nod, but his grip is so tight that I can't.

"Christ, woman. I don't know what I'm going to do with you."

He's already fucking my mouth even as he complains about it. And God, I love him like this. There's something so primal about being needed this way. I never want him not to need me this way. So I give myself over to it. Taking his cock as deep as I can, sucking and tasting him while my nails bite into the back of his muscular thighs.

We get lost in the rhythm, and I know when tension starts to ripple through his muscles, he's going to come. He tries to stop, presumably because he wants to fuck me, but I don't let him. I keep going until he's past the breaking point, hollowing my mouth around him as he starts to jerk, spilling his come between my lips.

I swallow what he has to give me, and when I'm done with that, I lick my lips and look up at him with a satisfactory grin.

"Jesus." He strokes my face beneath his fingers, his eyes on fire. "You're so goddamn beautiful, little monster. You're perfect in every way."

His words soak into my skin, warming me from the inside out. And then he has me on my back, his hands gliding beneath my skirt and dragging the material with it. When his head disappears beneath it, and he spreads me apart, I lay my head back with a contented sigh.

And then I count my blessings as he gives me the first of many orgasms for the night.

26

MERCEDES

"When hell freezes over," Georgie screeches, his upper lip curling in disgust as he stabs a finger at the diaper in Ivy's hand, "will I ever do that!"

Solana and I burst into a fit of laughter, my sides aching from possibly too much of a good thing, if that exists.

"Come on," Ivy implores him. "Just sniff it and take a guess."

"Absolutely not!" He shudders. "Nobody told me there would be torture involved at this party."

Solana snorts, and my eyes move to Judge, who seems to be firmly in Georgie's corner on this game. Santiago, too, is staring at his wife with wide, horrified eyes.

"Big babies!" Solana yells at them, her champagne nearly sloshing over the rim of her glass as she gestures across the room. "The whole lot of you. Ivy, bring that diaper to me. I'm about to show these men how it's done."

Ivy accepts gratefully, trudging over to Solana so she can sniff and take a guess. I'll admit, it wouldn't be my first choice of a game, but I know Ivy's worked really hard planning this, so I'm not about to tell her that. As the day got closer and she really threw herself into it, I realized that she never got to have these moments during her pregnancy. She missed out on so much. And quietly, I have made a promise that the next baby she and Santi have, I'm going to make sure she doesn't miss out on a single thing.

The diaper game continues, the women being the only good sports in the room until it comes time to measure my belly and take a guess at the circumference. Another horrifying game, but one the men seem to think they'll have in the bag.

"Remember, boys, you're calculating with real inches here." Solana wags a finger at them. "Not the generous measurements you'd give yourselves."

I roll my eyes and thank the Lord above when it's finally time for something I can sit back and enjoy. As it turns out, watching the men blindfolded and trying to put diapers on plastic dolls is quite entertaining. So much so that we're all in a fit of laughter by the time it's over.

The only one who seems to be taking it seriously, of course, is Judge. He's obviously been doing his homework, and I find the way he's concentrating so hard on everything to be equally hot and sweet. Now that I'm getting closer, I've sensed he's getting worried. But at the same time, he tries not to let it show. Yet I've found his stash of research in his study, printed packets of instruction manuals for first-time parents. He's even swiped a few of my books to read too.

I get why he's nervous because we'll be thrown in the deep end with twins. But oddly enough, I'm not that anxious anymore. Mostly, I'm just excited to meet them.

"Okay, okay." Ivy raises her hands, trying to quiet everyone. "It's time for the gender reveal."

This time, my stomach does do a little flip, and I know Judge feels the same when he comes to join me. With the assistance of Lois, Ivy wheels in the cart with the custom cake she ordered for the occasion. She's known since my last sonogram what the genders were, but Judge and I have been waiting for today to find out.

After a heated debate about which would be easier as first-time parents, boys or girls, we still haven't quite settled on a compromise. Regardless, we're about to find out what the reality is, and I know we'll both be happy whatever may come.

Ivy looks up at us, her excitement palpable as she asks, "Are you ready?"

"Yes," Judge answers for us both, trying to come off as cool and collected. Meanwhile, he's squeezing the life out of my hand.

Surprisingly, the room does actually fall into complete silence as Ivy cuts the cake, removing a perfect triangle to reveal a cascade of colorful candies. Only, there seems to be some confusion when we all notice there's both blue and pink.

"You're having one of each!" Ivy yells.

"Oh my god," I murmur as shouts erupt around us.

Judge turns my face to his, and the warmth in his eyes nearly makes me melt into the floor. He's never looked happier.

"One of each," he whispers against my lips. "I did that."

I smile against him and nod, giving him the credit he's weirdly proud of. "Yes, you did. Looks like it will be Ariana and Lawson, the second."

"Perfect." He drags my body closer still, his lips moving to my ear. "Now when is it appropriate to kick everyone out so I can take you to bed?"

At this, I do laugh. And I kiss him, getting so caught up in the moment, I almost forget about everyone else. That is until Santiago speaks.

"Seriously, Montgomery, get off my sister while you're in front of me. This is fucking weird."

Judge chuckles, reluctantly pulling away. The heat between us never quite dissipates, but we spend the rest of the evening with our family and friends. And I know without a doubt, I've never been happier either.

27

JUDGE

Late the next morning, I check on Mercedes. I slipped out of bed with the sun, but she didn't even stir. I know she must be exhausted. Like she said, her body is working hard to make two little humans. A boy and a girl. A bubble of something like happiness erupts in my chest at the thought. I close the door behind me, and she still doesn't move. She's in much the same position she was in when I left her earlier today, curled into where I was lying, her face on my pillow now, hand where my heart would be. She breathes quietly, expression relaxed, and it makes her look younger than she is.

I think about how she came to be here, in my house. In my keeping. How I took her from the compound bound and blindfolded. How I stripped her bare in every way and broke her in ways I didn't intend to. I think about how strong she was throughout all of it. All the humiliations, the hurt, the sadness, the pain, the attacks. How strong she is. Stronger than me, I think. I don't know if she realizes how much I learn from her as I consider how far she's come. Who she is now. Those women at The Society wouldn't recognize this Mercedes.

The truth be told, I've loved all the versions of her for a very long time. I just never realized having her was possible for me. I never considered it.

I shake my head at my own stupidity, thank the gods that she was able to overcome even that, and brush my lips over her forehead. I tuck the blanket around her shoulder, and I know it's not just exhaustion that has her sleeping so soundly. She's relaxing. Slowly but surely. In time, she will trust that we are meant to have a life together. To be happy. I will, too.

Quietly, I leave the bedroom. I'm on my way downstairs when my phone vibrates with a call. I slip it out of my pocket, see it's my brother, and answer. Even that says something. There was a time I'd ignore the call and send it directly to voicemail. Another thing to be grateful for is my cocky, arrogant brother, who almost died saving our lives. He will probably lord it over me for the rest of our days, but he will eventually walk out of that hospital. Not for a while yet and not without lasting scars both inside and out, but in time.

"Theron, good morning."

"Morning."

"Everything okay?" He doesn't usually call at this time.

"Yeah, fine. Everything's fine here." But I hear something in his tone. I'm about to ask what it is, but he continues. "Listen, I know she doesn't want me to tell you, but I think you should know."

I stop, wait.

"Mom was here. She left about half an hour ago."

"Our mother was there?" She has all but disappeared after her stunt of sending the bloody sheet to Santiago. Taunting him to get exactly the reaction she got.

"She didn't want me to tell you, obviously, but I have a feeling if I don't, she may be gone for good."

"Maybe she should be," I say, but I don't mean it. I know everything we've done, all the hurt we've caused, has come out of a past that molded us. Each one of us.

"You don't mean that, brother," he says. He knows me better than I give him credit for. "She's probably at the cottage by now. I doubt she'll stay long, so I'd suggest you make haste," he says. I hear two women's voices then wishing him a good morning, and I remember the scene when Mercedes and I visited, two pretty nurses tending to his every need. "Ladies," he says, his tone different when he's talking to them. I have to smile. It's good. It's what I'd asked for. That he survive. That he heal. That he walk away from this still intact. Himself. "I'll be right with you."

"Your entourage has arrived, I take it?"

"Something like that. Passes the time. You do what you want to do, but I thought you should know."

"Thank you."

We disconnect, and I slip the phone back into my pocket. Downstairs, I come across Lois and let her know Mercedes is still sleeping and shouldn't be disturbed. I'm about to go into my study to carry on with business as usual, but I stop at the door and change course. I head to my mother's cottage instead. Hers, too, allows for access from the back of the property. It's a longer way, but if you don't want to be seen from the main house, it does the trick. I find her car parked out front, the trunk open. One suitcase already inside.

Eyeing that, I climb the porch stairs and push open the door she's left slightly ajar. Inside the small kitchen, I find a large plain box on the table with an envelope set against it addressed to Mercedes and myself. I don't touch it, though, as I hear my mother's footfalls coming down the stairs. She's obviously carrying something heavy behind her. I hear the *thud thud thud* on the wooden steps.

She doesn't see me right away as she mutters a curse, the wheel of the suitcase she's bringing down having lodged itself between two of the rungs.

"Allow me," I say, and she jumps. I give her a smile, reaching over her to take hold of the suitcase as my mother puts a little space between us. I dislodge the suitcase and set it on the floor beside the other smaller one and turn to her.

My mother clears her throat, and I realize how much older she is. Still slender and petite. Still attractive. But older.

"Were you going to slip out in the night?"

She has the grace to lower her lashes, a flush creeping up her neck to her cheeks as she glances at the window. "Not in the night, no," she says, straightening to her full height of about five feet five inches and readying to face me.

I don't know what she's expecting. I'm not sure what I'm expecting. But I start. And I get right to it.

"What did you think to achieve sending that sheet to Santiago?" I hadn't even known it was gone. Mercedes told me later Miriam had changed the sheets, but I hadn't given it another thought.

She raises her chin. Aloof is always a defense she relies on. But her eyes give away the truth.

"I was just angry, Judge. So angry. I didn't know she was pregnant." Her shoulders slump, and she sets her hand on the back of one of the kitchen chairs.

I pull it out for her and then sit on one of the others, trying to set her at ease. I'm twice her size, and given my resemblance to my grandfather and our past, I'm sure she's intimidated. This is the most honest my mother has ever been with me. The most real. And I want to keep her talking.

She sits. "I knew her brother would take her away, and then maybe you and Theron could..." She trails off.

"Theron and I are going to be okay," I tell her.

Her eyes are wet when she looks at me. "When I heard what happened to him, and I was so far away, I almost died myself." I try not to let that sting. Theron did get the worst end of it. But she continues. "You and Mercedes too, you didn't deserve that. And I'm glad she and you and the babies are safe."

"Thank you. It is because of Theron."

She smiles a little proudly at that. "That's the Theron I know, Judge. It's the one you never knew." This gives me pause. All this time, all these years, has she had a piece of my brother that I refused to believe existed? How much time we've wasted. How much I've missed out on. We all have missed out on.

"I am sorry, if it makes any difference." She points at the envelope propped against the box on the table. "It's all in there. Along with some things for the baby I thought you might want. The christening gown both you and Theron wore, some keepsakes for the nursery, and just some other little things. You can throw it away. I'll understand."

"You kept all that?"

"Of course, I did. What mother wouldn't?"

I study her for a moment and absorb her words. We've been unfair to each other, but the past is past. It's time to let it go like I told Theron to do. "Where were you?"

She shrugs a shoulder. "I have a friend in Brazil."

My eyebrows shoot up. "Brazil?"

She smiles. "He's an old man. We've known each other for years, and well, it was past time I visited him, so I thought why not."

"Society?"

"No. The opposite. Just a simple, kind man whom I met when I was on a study trip a lifetime ago. We always returned to each other even after years without contact. A letter or a postcard, a photo maybe. His wife passed away a few years back, and honestly, I had no idea where else to go, but I knew I couldn't stay here."

"Because you were afraid of me. Of what you thought I'd do to you." The darkness that's always lurked beneath the surface swells a little as if her fear has given it breath. I tamp it down.

She just watches me but doesn't answer.

"I'm sorry I allowed him to do what he did to you. I'm sorry I stood by and watched. I'm sorry I didn't help you. And I'm sorry I didn't tell you this sooner."

Fat tears drop from her eyes. I reach for the box of tissues on the counter and hand her two. She takes them, thanks me, and blots at her eyes, careful of her makeup.

"You can stay," I tell her. "I'd like it if you did. I think Mercedes would like it, too."

"I'm not sure about that." She pushes to her feet. I do too.

"I am. Come to the house. Give us your gifts yourself."

"I have a flight to catch," she argues, but it's weak. I can see she wants to be here.

"Has your friend ever been to New Orleans?"

28

JUDGE

Mercedes goes into labor two weeks and a day before her due date.

"We should go," I tell her. I wanted to leave for the hospital hours ago, but she refused. She wanted to stay home as long as possible.

"Okay," she finally says, dragging herself out of bed. "Call Solana," she tells me as she walks toward the closet tugging at her nightie as she does. "She'll tell Georgie," she continues, having to pause to lean against the dresser when another contraction hits. "They'll meet us at the hospital. If you—" She stops speaking, squeezing her eyes shut as I wrap my arms around her. She leans into me.

"Mercedes." I hold her tight as her knees wobble with the pain that must be excruciating. I wish I could take it over from her.

"I need... my clothes." She points, taking a deep

breath in. The contraction has passed. I check my watch.

"You're not putting on clothes. There's no time." I wrap one of my sweaters over her shoulders and turn her to the door where the bag we packed waits, organized and ready for just this. "We need to get to the hospital."

"My shoes at least." She's wearing fluffy socks.

"You don't need them," I say and sweep her up in my arms. She doesn't fight me only because another contraction has her full attention.

Lois, who moved into the house a few weeks ago, opens her bedroom door. She's ready too.

"It's time?" she asks excitedly.

Mercedes makes a fist in my shirt, tugging hard enough to pull out some chest hair.

"It's time," I say. "Call the doctor and let him know we're coming."

"Wait, Judge, the suitcase," Lois says, rushing to grab it. How did I forget to take it? I literally just looked at it. But I'm a little out of sorts, I guess. Perhaps more than I realize.

"Don't forget to call Solana!" Mercedes demands as she manages the pain of the contraction.

"Yes, and let Solana know it's time," I repeat to Lois although I'm sure she heard. "Raul!" I call out on our way down the stairs. Raul is tugging on his jacket, keys in hand. He, too, has moved into the house for just this event.

"Fuck, it hurts," Mercedes manages when she gets a breath. I've been watching her for hours, keeping track of the time between contractions. Hating that I can't do anything to help her. But if I thought it was bad before, I was mistaken.

"It's going to be okay," I try to reassure calmly as I get her into the car and slide in beside her. Raul rushes us down the lane of oaks and out the gates toward the hospital as Mercedes curls into me again, moaning in pain as I rub her back, feeling pathetically helpless and completely powerless.

"Jesus. I'm going to die," she says.

"No. I won't let you."

"Fuck!"

"We're supposed to breathe," I tell her, remembering what I'd read, what the woman at the birthing classes said. Or is it count? Are we supposed to fucking count? Fuck. I can't remember.

Her body relaxes a little as the contraction passes, and when she looks up at me, I see how her hair is sticking to her forehead. I wipe tears from her eyes.

"Breathe. It's supposed to help. Deep breath in, deep breath out. Do it with me, Mercedes. Breathe with me."

"I am breathing." Her face contorts with the next wave of pain.

"Do it with me. I'll count—"

She fists my shirt again, and I lean toward her to

alleviate some of the pain. "I am fucking breathing, you asshole!"

"She said it would relax you."

"She's a fucking liar!"

"Raul?" I call out without looking away from her.

"I'm going as fast as I can." He swerves around a street sweeper who honks his horn at us.

"Oh shit, oh shit, oh shit!"

"What? What is it?" I ask as Mercedes sits up a little and looks down at the little bit of water on the leather seat that grows before my eyes. Oh fuck.

"Shit!"

"It's okay. Your water broke. That's all," I say in a tone intended to calm and reassure her.

"That's all?" She starts to grow angry, but her pain mutes her.

"Raul, are we fucking there?" I snap at him before turning more gently to her. "It's fine, sweetheart. It's fine."

Raul takes a sharp turn into the parking lot as Mercedes lets out an ear-piercing cry and doubles over.

"They're going to fucking kill me."

"We're here, honey. We're here. We'll get that epidural first thing."

"No! I said no epidural!" She turns feral eyes to me. "Do you ever fucking listen?"

"That's right. I'm sorry. I forgot. I was just trying to help. I—"

She clutches my shirt again as two nurses appear at my door that Raul opens. They have a wheelchair ready but get one look at Mercedes, who honestly looks a little wild, and turn to me for instruction.

"Honey," I start. "Let's get you in that chair so the nurses can—"

"If you call me honey or sweetheart one more fucking time, I'm going to kill you. Get the fuck out of my way!"

I nod, hearing Raul's chuckle, which he's quick to hide when I look his way, and help my wife out of the car and into the wheelchair.

"No epidural," I tell the nurses as we rush in. "It's in her birth plan. I have it..." I look around, realizing I must have still forgotten the case. I set it down to get her into the car. It's probably still just outside the house.

"Yes, epidural. I changed my mind!" Mercedes yells.

"It's the pain talking," I tell the nurses. "She was adamant—"

Mercedes swivels her head toward me *Exorcist*-like, and I shut my mouth. "You fucking asshole," she says, voice low and a little terrifying. "I am birthing not one but two of your little monsters. You think you can dictate if I get a fucking epidural?"

"No, sweetheart. You can get what you want. Anything you want." Because right now, I'm honestly a little afraid of her.

She nods as the nurses wheel her into her private room. It's the one we arranged for, another perk of The Society. I stand back as her doctor rushes through the door and watch, stunned, from my place in the corner as they get her set up and the doctor checks how far she is.

Another contraction hits, and I want to warn the doctor, but she seems unfazed.

"Judge!" Mercedes calls out, extending her hand.

I hurry to her side and hold on to her, kissing her forehead, wiping away the sweat.

"You're halfway there, Mercedes," the doctor happily announces, standing and wiping off her hands. She then gets a look at my wife's face.

"Halfway? Are you kidding?"

The woman looks at me, but just then, Solana comes flying through the door, and Mercedes seems relieved. Solana goes to her other side and hugs her, placing her bag down. She takes candles from it, setting them on the table beside the bed while talking quietly to Mercedes, who seems to be listening and calming.

"Where's the music?" Solana asks me after a quick search of the room.

"I forgot the suitcase," I confess.

"You forgot the suitcase?" Mercedes explodes. "You had one thing to do. One thing while I push your babies out of my body, and you *forgot*?"

Solana grins happily. "It's okay, sweetie. I have us

covered." She reaches once again into her giant bag and produces a small speaker. A moment later, soothing New Age music is playing. She holds my gaze over Mercedes's head but addresses Mercedes. "Why is it the men are so big and strong while depositing their seed but go green when the time comes to reap what they sow?"

Mercedes looks up at me and laughs, then cries with the pain of a new contraction.

"Judge, go get her some ice chips. Go on. Out."

I nod, grateful to Solana, and find Georgie outside. He takes one look at me, and I wonder if I look like he does. Pale and completely out of our element.

"Ice chips?" I ask him. Why do I ask him?

"Ice chips. Yes. I'll ask a nurse." He goes to the station, and I see how his hair is ruffled, and he must have pulled clothes on over top of his pajamas. I look down at myself. I am wearing jeans and a shirt that's wrinkled from Mercedes twisting it and from me sleeping in it. I wanted to be ready to go, so I've been sleeping fully dressed for the past week. Mercedes laughed at the idea.

A nurse returns with Georgie. She takes a look at me and grins knowingly. "Here you go. Your wife will be grateful for these."

"Thank you," I say, taking the cup. "You coming?" I ask Georgie wondering why the fuck I'm asking him. Almost as though he'd be my ally.

"Hell no. I hear her fine from out here."

The nurse chuckles, and I reenter the room where, over the next few hours, Mercedes goes through what I can imagine to be horrific pain without agreeing to the epidural I would have taken hours ago. I know she's hoping for a natural birth without a C-section, which may not be possible with twins. But I don't know why I even think that when I hear the first little cry of a brand-new voice. Because if anyone can do this, can bend fate to their will, it's my wife.

And as Ariana is handed to me while the doctor attends to her brother, I feel my own eyes well with emotion.

Lawson joins us just moments later, and it's as though he's searching for his sister, desperate to be reunited with her because he wails, his little face bright pink with anger until they are weighed, wiped down, and swaddled, then laid on their mother's breast where he worms his spindly little arm out of the swaddle to lay his hand on his sister's cheek.

It's only then they quiet. And fuck. It's the most beautiful thing I have ever seen in my life.

29

JUDGE

Several months later

It's late when Santiago and I walk into Hildebrand's office at The Tribunal building. Tomorrow, Mercedes and I leave on our honeymoon along with our entire extended, somewhat dysfunctional family. Not how I expected to spend my honeymoon, but I wouldn't have it any other way. And I am determined not to let Hildebrand's dour face and demeanor cloud even one second of it. Mercedes and I have traveled a very long, very hard road to get here. And now that we've arrived, I won't allow anyone to cast their shadow over our family, our future, or our happiness.

"Judge, Santiago," Hildebrand says, standing to

greet us with a smile I've come to know. It's the one you never see standing before the three Councilors of The Tribunal when they are seated in official robes. He reserves this smile for when he knows the playing ground is level. Because Councilor Hildebrand does not like a level playing field. Never has.

"Councilor," Santiago says dismissively. I wonder which of us likes this man less.

"Hildebrand," I greet with a nod, choosing not to use the title he is too happy with.

His eyes narrow infinitesimally, but he forces that smile to widen and directs us to have a seat in the two chairs set before his desk. He is so calculated, even switching out furnishings depending on the situation and, even more importantly, the visitor.

"I thought you'd be coming alone, Judge."

"Considering it was my sister's wedding that was crashed, and she was the target, I felt it more than appropriate I be present," Santiago answers before I can.

"Well, yes, of course. But Mr. Montgomery and I have some Tribunal business to discuss—"

"Nothing that can't be discussed in front of my brother-in-law," I tell him. I will keep no more secrets from my friend.

Hildebrand gives a disapproving exhale and settles into his chair, which is like a throne behind his desk. He wants me to sit as a Councilor on The Tribunal. And as I watch him I wonder more and more if the course my grandfather and Hildebrand set for me isn't where I'll do the most good. If I do it, though, it will be on my terms.

"First, allow me to congratulate you on your nuptials and the birth of your children, Judge," Hildebrand starts. He takes a small box out of his desk drawer and pushes it toward me. "For your daughter." The IVI bracelet all girls are gifted upon birth.

"Thank you," I say, leaving the box where it is. I'll take it home, but I can't guarantee Ariana will be wearing it anytime soon. I'll leave that to Mercedes to decide. Because ultimately, it's a mark of ownership already. My daughter is a member of our Society, even if she is a Sovereign daughter. And that means something. And then there's my son. A Sovereign Son like myself. Like Santiago and even Hildebrand. Privileged beyond belief. The world open to him. To her, too, but to a lesser extent.

"I trust you are fully recovered from the unfortunate incident earlier this year, Judge?"

The unfortunate incident of him requiring the full extent of punishment for Mercedes's role in bringing unwanted attention to The Society. For my invoking the Vicarius clause and taking that punishment over.

"I am, thank you for your concern." He is not concerned. It's that playing field he would like to tip in his favor.

"Now that we've dispatched with the pleasantries," Santiago starts, emphasizing the word pleasantries. "Perhaps you can tell me how an armed outsider managed to get on IVI grounds on the night of my sister's wedding and attempt to kill her, succeed in almost killing her husband and her brother-in-law, who, by the way, was the man who brought Vincent Douglas down. Not an IVI guard of whom there were plenty."

"What are you suggesting, Mr. De La Rosa?"

"I'm not suggesting anything. I'd just like to know what the hell happened that night."

Hildebrand takes a moment but then nods. "As would I. We've questioned the guards at the gates, and two have been disciplined."

"Two? What about the others?" I ask.

He glances at his desk, then back up at me. "I understand your brother needed long-term rehabilitation. I'm sure those costs are exorbitant. We will, of course, pay for his treatment and any distress the situation caused him."

"Money is not the issue, Councilor. I'd prefer you take responsibility for what happened. More people could have been hurt if not for my brother."

"Yes, Theron did a service to the Society," he agrees. "And for that, he shall be rewarded."

"You and Theron can work out those details between yourselves another time. But The Tribunal's role, considering it is The Tribunal who manages security for our members, is what I'd like to discuss tonight."

He clears his throat, struggling with this part. But neither Santiago nor I plan to let him off the hook, and we sit quietly, letting time do its work.

"I believe, gentlemen, that it came down to one thing. Vincent Douglas was determined to avenge his sister's death. And we as The Tribunal underestimated his determination."

"And my pregnant wife was almost killed for it!" I slam a fist on his desk.

Both Hildebrand's guard and Santiago are on their feet in an instant, each with a hand on my shoulder. I realize I'm up towering over the older man. And Hildebrand looks more afraid than I've ever seen him.

I draw a deep breath in and manage my rage.

"Judge," Santiago says quietly, gesturing for me to sit.

I do. And again, we wait for Hildebrand as he instructs his guard to leave the room. No witnesses, I guess. Once the guard is gone, he clears his throat and starts.

"The oversight was ours. And The Tribunal apologizes for any inconvenience."

"You must agree it was more than an inconvenience, Councilor," Santiago says through gritted teeth.

"Yes, it was. You have our sincerest apology." He

tilts his head, hating this. "But, Judge, since you mention your wife's pregnancy. She was impregnated while in your care under the Rite, isn't that correct?" he asks me with a pointed glance at Santiago.

"That matter is not for you to consider, Councilor," I say calmly. Even if Santiago has forgiven me, I should have done better and been more trustworthy. Done things the correct way with Mercedes.

"Well, perhaps her brother would like it considered."

"They are married. My sister is happy," Santiago says. "And I am very pleased to call Judge my brother." Santiago looks at me, and I feel a rush of emotion at his words. He turns back to Hildebrand. "That is all that matters."

"IVI will need to move toward adopting more modern thinking on such matters, don't you think, Councilor?" I ask.

He raises his eyebrows.

"It's one of the initiatives I plan to pursue once I'm seated on The Tribunal."

This stops him, and I see what I believe to be as authentic a smile as he can muster. "Well, Judge, this is good news."

I'm sure he still believes the power of being a councilor will corrupt me. I have no intention of allowing it to turn me into someone like him.

"I've already spoken with Montrose privately.

Once he steps down in a few years' time, I will take his place."

"A few years?" The pleased smile is gone.

"He is not ready to go, and a seat on The Tribunal is a lifetime appointment. As you say yourself, the law must be followed to the letter." Those were his exact words when he'd ordered my brutal lashing.

"Yes, that's true, isn't it? What are we if we cannot follow our own laws."

"Exactly."

I check my watch and stand. "It's late. We don't want to keep you, and we have an early morning, don't we?" I ask Santiago.

"We do, and if I am not home to assist Ivy in packing, I will not hear the end of it."

"I'll be sure Theron touches base with you regarding that compensation once he's home."

"I look forward to it," Hildebrand says, extending a hand to me.

I look at it, and I take it. Because it's all you can do with men like him. Keep them close. Keep balance on that playing field.

"Enjoy your honeymoon, Judge," he says.

"Thank you, Councilor."

EPILOGUE
MERCEDES

"Is everything to your liking, Mr. Montgomery?"

The stewardess eyes my husband like he's a cool drink on a hot summer day. It's the same way she's been eyeing him all week, and I don't like it. I don't like it one fucking bit. Yet there's something to be said because Judge doesn't take his eyes off me as he responds.

"Everything is perfect." His hand skims up over my thigh beneath the table, fingers warming my sun-kissed skin.

The stewardess lingers, waiting for his eyes to catch hers, but they never do.

"That will be all." I grin at her, all teeth. "Unless there's something else you'd like to ask my husband?"

She blanches, shaking her head quickly, and then scurries off.

"I swear to God," I grumble as I squeeze Judge's ridiculously handsome face between my palms. "I can't take you anywhere."

"Oh, I don't think that's true." He leans closer, his lips brushing against mine. "I rather like seeing you this way."

"Is that so?" I smile at him sweetly.

He nods, his hand skating further up my thigh. His eyes are dark and hot, and it wouldn't take much to lure him below deck right now. But if there's one thing that hasn't changed, it's that Judge and I still like to play games. We just play them a little differently now.

"Seriously," Santi groans, interrupting that thought. "What have I told you about groping my sister at the breakfast table?"

"It's our honeymoon," Judge reminds him. "What did you expect?"

Another grunt. "I'm only here because my wife insisted we needed to come."

As soon as the words leave his mouth, Ivy appears from the main salon looking freshly fucked and pleased as hell.

"It doesn't look like you're faring too badly yourself," Judge remarks dryly.

"Okay now it's my turn to gag." I grab my mimosa and take a long sip.

Santi gives me a roguish grin and shrugs apologetically, except I know he's not sorry. Not one bit.

In addition to Santi and Ivy crashing our honeymoon, Solana, Georgie, Lois, and even Theron are here too. It's either the craziest idea we've ever had or the best. Because with the exception of Theron, who I still trust about as far as I can throw him, they've all been taking turns helping with the babies. Which means Judge and I have the best of both worlds. Because there was no way we were leaving them anywhere while we jetted off to some beautiful destination. But Judge insisted he was giving me a honeymoon, and he's come through on that promise while giving me something that I need just as much. Time with our friends and family.

We've been lazing our days away on a yacht somewhere in the Mediterranean, cruising from one beautiful port to the next. It's been over a week of sun, sea, and hot sex, and I wouldn't have it any other way.

"Ugggg." Solana groans as she finally decides to join us, her hair tossed up in a messy bun and huge sunglasses covering her eyes.

It doesn't escape anyone's notice that Theron's eyes go straight to her ass as she moves across the deck. I shoot him a glare, and he shrugs.

"Where are we even at?" Solana asks. "Or better yet, what day is it?"

"It's punishment day, from the looks of it," I tell

her. "That's what you get for playing drinking games all night."

"It's Georgie's fault." She plunks into a chair at the table and pours herself some coffee. "He's the one who wanted to do karaoke."

"Which was riveting," Judge says dryly. "Please, give us another rendition this evening."

Solana rolls her eyes. "As if you were even there. Don't think I didn't notice you hauling your wife off to your stateroom, Lawson Montgomery."

"I won't deny it," he says smoothly.

"Where are my babies?" Solana pouts.

"Sleeping. And don't you dare think about waking them up," I tell her. "Lois will murder you if I don't."

She wrinkles her nose at me. "I can't help it. They are so cute."

"I make good babies," Judge says proudly.

I shoot him a glare. "Oh, you make good babies, all on your own, huh?"

He arches a brow at me, amused. "I'm having flashbacks of the delivery."

"You're just lucky they have my lovely temperament."

At this, he snorts. "Temper is more like it."

I flash him another sweet smile, and he leans in to kiss my jaw before whispering in my ear.

"Should I work on putting another one in you?"

"Lawson Montgomery, don't you dare utter those words to me for at least another five years."

He chuckles, his fingers moving to the nape of my neck, settling on the tattoo he finally inked into my skin. It took us some time to adjust to our new schedule of caring for the twins at all hours of the night, and it didn't come without its struggles. Judge still shudders every time he refers to that period as the ice age because I was hormonal and, quite frankly, overwhelmed. I cried often and took out my frustrations on him even more often, but through it all, he was there. He talked me through the rough nights, held me through the worst ones, and put up with enough to make him look like a saint. And for that, I love him even more.

It took some time for us to come back to ourselves and figure out how to navigate parenthood with marriage. At times, it felt like we were both fumbling around in the dark, but we got through it. We're still getting through it. And when it felt like we'd finally weathered the worst of the storm, I asked Judge to do what he'd set out to the night he married me.

So in a courtyard full of our family and friends, and a horde of guards with weapons this time, I kneeled before him and let him ink his family crest into my skin. Honestly, I don't think there's ever been anything hotter, and he thought so too, if the way he spent the rest of the night inside me is any indication.

Now, every time he touches it, I feel that possession. His claim on me. And maybe it's an antiquated tradition, but I like having his brand on me. I love it, in fact. It's almost ironic, considering I spent my whole life trying to escape these customs. Now, I'm in it for the long haul. But it doesn't scare me the way it once did. There's something freeing about being with Judge in this capacity. He's still the same bossy, domineering man who boils my blood at times. And with my temper, there's never a lack of passion between us. But I love my life. I love my husband. Our babies. Our beautiful, dysfunctional family. We have more than any two people should have, and I'll never stop being grateful for it. Not for one second.

Yet sometimes, I still can't help myself. I have to keep Judge on his toes. Which is exactly what I intend to do when the deckhand makes an appearance. He's a young, handsome Frenchman who's charming as hell. Of course, he doesn't hold a candle to Judge, and he never will. But that's beside the point.

"It feels hot outside today, doesn't it?" I ask Solana.

I can't see her eyes behind the big sunglasses, but a smile curves her lips as she catches my drift. "It does. I think it's going to be a scorcher."

"Mercedes." Judge's voice is a low growl in my ear that I ignore.

"I could almost use a dip." I lean into him and give him a chaste kiss on the cheek before I'm up on my feet.

I can hear his muttered curse from under his breath as I walk toward the swim deck, unknotting my sarong and letting it fall away. Underneath, I'm wearing a black bikini. The result of a lot of time in the aerial studio. My body probably won't ever be the same, considering I have hips and an ass now, but I'm happy in my skin, scars and all, and nothing can take that away.

"Hey, Philippe." I wave up at the deckhand with a dazzling smile.

"Hello, Mrs. Montgomery." He dips his head politely, but his gaze lingers for a minute.

That's about the time an arm catches me around the waist, and I let out a squeak of feigned surprise.

"What are you doing, little monster?" Judge whispers in that low voice full of dark promises.

"What?" I return innocently.

"You know what." He slaps my ass in front of everyone, and heat flushes my cheeks.

"I don't know. I rather like seeing you this way." I turn his earlier words around on him.

He offers me a devilish grin, sliding his tongue over his teeth. "Is that so?"

I nod.

"Well, in that case..." He scoops me up over his shoulder, and I squeal for real this time as he carries me off caveman style toward our room. "I think it's time to remind you who you belong to, Mrs. Montgomery."

A secret smile curves my face as I bob up and down, waving goodbye to the laughing faces at the breakfast table. "As if I could ever forget."

WHAT TO READ NEXT
REQUIEM OF THE SOUL

Requiem of the Soul is the first book set in the world of The Society. If you enjoyed this book and are new to The Society, you can continue your journey here.

Welcome to The Society...

The lace of my dress scratches my skin. I shiver. It's cold, a wet cold as soft mist turns to rain. Rain on your wedding day is good luck, right? Isn't that what they say?

Candles protected inside glass lanterns line the stairs leading up to the double front doors. I stare up at them, remembering the last time I stood here. It's been a while.

The doors are opened. Organ music and incense pour out.

I close my eyes, listening to the sound, and take a deep breath. The scent and sound combined are dizzying.

No, it's not those things that have me swaying on my feet. It's what's coming. What's waiting for me at the end of the aisle.

My brother wraps his hand around my arm. He mutters a curse as he rights me.

I grip my bouquet of blood-red roses. If I'm not careful, I'll crush them. They're striking. Beautiful. Like my dress. He has impeccable taste, my fiancé, and he likes things a certain way. He has rules. And he's used to getting exactly what he wants.

I'm slow as we ascend the stairs toward the entrance. It irritates my brother, I know, but everything irritates him. The toe of his shoe catches my long veil, tugging my head backward momentarily. A few steps more and we stand inside the vestibule, the organ louder, the incense stronger, combining with the smell of melting wax.

The doors close behind us, that final divide between what was and what will be. My past and my present. The voice inside my head urging me to run grows louder, but I don't run. It's no use.

Our guests rise to their feet, gazes blank as they turn back to look at me, their sacrificial bride. I don't see their faces, though. They're just shapes in my periphery. I only have eyes for one man. The stranger before the altar. The stranger in whose bed I'll sleep tonight.

I feel numb. Like it's not real. Like it's not me.

The room sways, and my brother's grip tightens. I'll have a bruise tomorrow. We take one step then another. I clutch my bouquet like it's my lifeline. My nails break the skin of my palms, the blood slippery, wet, the pain keeping me from giving in to the vertigo.

A thousand candles bathe the cathedral in a soft glow, the music more fitting for a Requiem Mass than a wedding march. I guess he chose that too. It goes with the dress at least. My fiancé's doing. I understand why.

My eyes lock on him. He's half-turned toward us, watching us.

My brother walks me past our guests. I only recognize one or two. All men. Only men. A dozen of them. My own mother is absent. I glance at my brother, see a dark smear of dirt or blood on his collar. I hadn't noticed it before, and I want to ask what it is but don't. His jaw is set, eyes hard. It should have been my father walking me down the aisle, but he can't do that.

Sadness washes over me, but I don't have time for it. Not here. Not now. Because we're almost there.

I look down at the polished marble floor cold against my bare feet, and I take my final steps to the altar where every sound is amplified in this strange dream that is somehow my reality.

My brother turns me to face him. He lifts the veil, then leans down to brush his cold cheek against mine. My eyes lock on my fiancé over his shoulder. His face is still in shadows, but he's watching us. Watching me. I see the glint of hazel eyes.

Santiago De La Rosa.

The man who has chosen me for his wife.

The man to whom I will belong.

My brother straightens. With a tug, he offers my hand to Santiago.

I swallow hard, my heart pounding against my chest, and when Santiago takes my wrist, the flowers slip from my grasp to scatter at our feet, blood-red against the stark, cold marble.

I barely notice because I am riveted.

Because that's when the candles flicker, sending light and shadows dancing across his face, and I get my first real glimpse of him. My breath catches in my throat, the gasp drowned out by the organ, by the sound of the priest telling the witnesses to be seated, and the creaking of the ancient pews as the ceremony begins.

ALSO BY A. ZAVARELLI

Kingdom Fall

A Sovereign Sons Novel

The Society Trilogy

Requiem of the Soul

Reparation of Sin

Resurrection of the Heart

Ties that Bind Duet

Mine

His

Boston Underworld Series

Crow

Reaper

Ghost

Saint

Thief

Conor

Sin City Salvation Series

Confess

Convict

Bleeding Hearts Series

Echo

Stutter

Standalones

Stealing Cinderella

Beast

Pretty When She Cries

Tap Left

Hate Crush

For a complete list of books and audios, visit http://www.azavarelli.com/books

ALSO BY NATASHA KNIGHT

The Rite Trilogy

His Rule

Her Rebellion

Their Reign

The Devil's Pawn Duet

Devil's Pawn

Devil's Redemption

To Have and To Hold

With This Ring

I Thee Take

Stolen: Dante's Vow

The Society Trilogy

Requiem of the Soul

Reparation of Sin

Resurrection of the Heart

Dark Legacy Trilogy

Taken (Dark Legacy, Book 1)

Torn (Dark Legacy, Book 2)

Twisted (Dark Legacy, Book 3)

Unholy Union Duet

Unholy Union

Unholy Intent

Collateral Damage Duet

Collateral: an Arranged Marriage Mafia Romance

Damage: an Arranged Marriage Mafia Romance

Ties that Bind Duet

Mine

His

MacLeod Brothers

Devil's Bargain

Benedetti Mafia World

Salvatore: a Dark Mafia Romance

Dominic: a Dark Mafia Romance

Sergio: a Dark Mafia Romance

The Benedetti Brothers Box Set (Contains Salvatore, Dominic and Sergio)

Killian: a Dark Mafia Romance

Giovanni: a Dark Mafia Romance

The Amado Brothers

Dishonorable

Disgraced

Unhinged

Standalone Dark Romance

Descent

Deviant

Beautiful Liar

Retribution

Theirs To Take

Captive, Mine

Alpha

Given to the Savage

Taken by the Beast

Claimed by the Beast

Captive's Desire

Protective Custody

Amy's Strict Doctor

Taming Emma

Taming Megan

Taming Naia

Reclaiming Sophie

The Firefighter's Girl

Dangerous Defiance

Her Rogue Knight

Taught To Kneel

Tamed: the Roark Brothers Trilogy

THANK YOU

Thanks for reading *The Rite Trilogy*. We hope you loved Mercedes and Judge's wild romance!

ABOUT NATASHA KNIGHT

Natasha Knight is the *USA Today* Bestselling author of Romantic Suspense and Dark Romance Novels. She has sold over a million books and is translated into six languages. She currently lives in The Netherlands with her husband and two daughters and when she's not writing, she's walking in the woods listening to a book, sitting in a corner reading or off exploring the world as often as she can get away.

Write Natasha here: natasha@natasha-knight.com

www.natasha-knight.com

ABOUT A. ZAVARELLI

A. Zavarelli is a USA Today and Amazon bestselling author of dark and contemporary romance.

When she's not putting her characters through hell, she can usually be found watching bizarre and twisted documentaries in the name of research.

She currently lives in the Northwest with her lumberjack and an entire brood of fur babies.

Want to stay up to date on Ashleigh and Natasha's releases? Sign up for our newsletters here: https://landing.mailerlite.com/webforms/landing/x3sok6

Printed in Great Britain
by Amazon